LILACS BY THE SEA

BLUE HERON COTTAGES
BOOK FIVE

KAY CORRELL

ZURA LU PUBLISHING LLC

Published by Zura Lu Publishing LLC

ABOUT THIS BOOK

Francine Winters—Frankie to her family and friends—doesn't know how she got to this point in her life. Her marriage is falling apart. Will moved into the guest bedroom and their marriage is crumbling.

They're considering a trial separation but haven't told their grown daughters yet.

Which is too bad because...

The last thing she needs is the surprise family vacation the girls plan.

And to make things worse? They planned it at the very place she and Will had honeymooned. A celebration for their fortieth anniversary.

Frankie is sure she can make it through this. It's only one week, right? Then they'll tell their daughters the truth.

But a lot can happen when you come to stay at
Blue Heron Cottages…

This book is dedicated to all the workers who tirelessly toiled to help clean up after Hurricane Ian. I'm forever grateful the storm mostly spared our home and my heart goes out to those who lost everything.

KAY'S BOOKS

Find more information on all my books at
kaycorrell.com

COMFORT CROSSING ~ THE SERIES

The Shop on Main - Book One

The Memory Box - Book Two

The Christmas Cottage - A Holiday Novella
(Book 2.5)

The Letter - Book Three

The Christmas Scarf - A Holiday Novella
(Book 3.5)

The Magnolia Cafe - Book Four

The Unexpected Wedding - Book Five

The Wedding in the Grove - (a crossover short

story between series - with Josephine and Paul from The Letter.)

LIGHTHOUSE POINT ~ THE SERIES

Wish Upon a Shell - Book One

Wedding on the Beach - Book Two

Love at the Lighthouse - Book Three

Cottage near the Point - Book Four

Return to the Island - Book Five

Bungalow by the Bay - Book Six

Christmas Comes to Lighthouse Point - Book Seven

CHARMING INN ~ Return to Lighthouse Point

One Simple Wish - Book One

Two of a Kind - Book Two

Three Little Things - Book Three

Four Short Weeks - Book Four

Five Years or So - Book Five

Six Hours Away - Book Six

Charming Christmas - Book Seven

SWEET RIVER ~ THE SERIES

A Dream to Believe in - Book One

A Memory to Cherish - Book Two

A Song to Remember - Book Three

A Time to Forgive - Book Four

A Summer of Secrets - Book Five

A Moment in the Moonlight - Book Six

MOONBEAM BAY ~ THE SERIES

The Parker Women - Book One

The Parker Cafe - Book Two

A Heather Parker Original - Book Three

The Parker Family Secret - Book Four

Grace Parker's Peach Pie - Book Five

The Perks of Being a Parker - Book Six

BLUE HERON COTTAGES ~ THE SERIES

Memories of the Beach - Book One

Walks along the Shore - Book Two

Bookshop near the Coast - Book Three

Restaurant on the Wharf - Book Four

Lilacs by the Sea - Book Five

Flower Shop on Magnolia - Book Six

More to come!

WIND CHIME BEACH ~ A stand-alone novel

INDIGO BAY ~ A multi-author sweet romance series

Sweet Days by the Bay - Kay's Complete Collection of stories in the Indigo Bay series

Sign up for my newsletter at my website *kaycorrell.com* to make sure you don't miss any new releases or sales.

CHAPTER 1

F rancine Winters tossed a suitcase on the bed, spreading both sides open like wings. Packing for a trip to the beach was the last thing in the world she wanted to be doing right now. But it couldn't be helped. She couldn't disappoint her daughters.

She grabbed two sundresses and her favorite pair of capri pants from the walk-in closet, ignoring the one long, empty side. There was no reason she shouldn't spread out her things and take over that side of the closet, and yet, she hadn't.

She walked back to the bed and carefully folded each item before placing them in the suitcase. Her daughters had suggested she find a fancy dress for the celebration, but she hadn't found the time. Or, more honestly, she hadn't wanted to go shopping. Not for a dress she'd wear one time and then give away because she surely wouldn't want to keep it and the memories attached to it.

How had she let herself be talked into the whole ordeal? But she could do it, couldn't she? Just seven days.

Seven days of pretending.

Seven days of lying to her daughters.

Her heart skipped a beat. She wasn't one for telling lies, even if it was a lie of omission. But two weeks ago, when her daughters surprised her and her husband, Will, with this trip, neither of them had the heart to tell the girls no.

A celebration of forty years of marriage. Their anniversary. But that didn't really matter now, did it? Well, it mattered. They had two wonderful daughters together.

She and Will had actually asked the girls over that night to tell them things were going to be different. That Will was moving out—not that he'd actually found a place yet. But then the girls sprang the trip on them, and neither one of them wanted to disappoint their daughters. So here she was. Packing for a family vacation ending with a fancy dinner on their fortieth anniversary.

She closed her eyes for a moment, overwhelmed by the mere thought of the coming week. She sensed it more than heard as Will stepped into the bedroom. She opened her eyes and turned slowly around.

"Frankie, you about packed?" He stood awkwardly in the doorway.

"No, not yet."

"I… uh… I need something from the bottom drawer of the dresser. Guess I didn't get all my things out of here."

She nodded as he walked over to the heavy, dark cherry dresser and opened one of the bottom drawers. He'd always used the bottom drawers and left the top ones with easy access for her. He pulled out a couple of folded t-shirts and stood up straight. "Sorry." The pain in his eyes was only thinly veiled.

"No, that's fine."

"We'll drive together?" He cocked his head to one side, his eyes questioning her. And that was a change. Will was always certain of

3

himself, of his decisions. Of… everything. But not so much in the last six months or so.

"Of course. Yes. Together. I'll be ready in twenty minutes." It would be silly to drive separate cars—not to mention awkward if the girls found out. But this meant she had a bit over an hour in the car with Will. Longer than they'd been together, just the two of them, in months.

Will nodded and disappeared out the door, his footsteps echoing on the wooden floor as he walked toward the guest bedroom. Her heart squeezed in her chest, and the enormity of the ruse they had to maintain this week suffocated her.

Maybe they should have just told the girls the truth.

But they'd been so excited about this trip. Both had taken the week off from work. Katie probably made most of the plans. Her oldest daughter was a planner, a doer. Her younger daughter, Stacey, always went along with whatever Katie wanted. It had always been that way. She wondered, often, why neither of them was married. Neither of them had given her the grandchildren she thought she'd have by now.

The ones she would read to and take to the park and teach how to swim in their pool.

But no babies, no spouses. Well, Stacey had been married for a brief period in her early twenties, but that marriage crashed and burned a fiery death within six months.

Frankie thought she'd given them an excellent role model of a perfect marriage. Caring parents. Involved in their lives, their studies, and the sports they played. Going to teacher conferences and taking them on yearly family vacations. The perfect family life, right?

Well, at least until this last year. But the girls knew nothing about that. And they weren't going to hear about it this week, either. Both she and Will agreed with that. Plenty of time to tell the girls after they got back from their trip.

But they would have to tell them before the Thanksgiving and Christmas holidays came around. She couldn't bear to put up a charade for the holidays. They'd have to figure out some way to handle all that. Maybe they could do Thanksgiving with their father and Christmas with her?

The magnitude of the impending changes sucked the breath out of her when she thought about it. But now wasn't the time to think about it. Now was the time to march into the bathroom and get her makeup and curling iron. Grab her favorite face lotion and hairbrush. Finish packing and get going.

She should have packed last night and given herself more time to make choices. Decide what to wear. What to bring. But last night she'd sat alone in the large, king-sized bed and eaten a pint of cookies-and-cream ice cream instead of dealing with the packing as if that would make the whole week disappear.

It hadn't.

She looked in the mirror and put on a practiced smile. Did it look genuine? Maybe, if no one looked at her eyes.

Will disagreed with Frankie's decision to not tell the girls about their separation. But Frankie was so adamant about it. He was having the hardest time figuring out this woman he'd been married to for almost forty years. He thought he knew everything about her. What she liked. What she didn't like. What she was thinking. But now?

Now he never knew anything and walked around on eggshells trying not to irritate her—or worse, disappoint her.

He let out a long sigh as he shoved the t-shirts he'd retrieved from their bedroom—no, *Frankie's* bedroom—into his suitcase. The girls were terribly excited about this big surprise trip they'd planned for the anniversary. He'd do his best to act like everything was normal.

But it wasn't. Not even a little. After all this time, Frankie wanted…

What did she want? She'd said she was unhappy. Okay, he could see that. Clearly see that. She said she needed time on her own.

She hadn't gone so far as to say she didn't love him anymore… but did she? Love him?

There was no denying they'd drifted apart after the girls grew up and moved out. It was like all the girls' activities had kept them bonded. Kept them close. And his job had taken off at the exact time the girls moved out. He was often out of town for weeks at a time with crazy long hours.

The first few years after the girls left, Frankie was miserable and waited impatiently for them to visit. She threw herself into Stacey's wedding,

KAY CORRELL

and then that marriage imploded. Not that it was surprising, really. He never knew what Stacey saw in the guy. All Stacey and her husband did was argue. Constantly.

He and Frankie didn't argue. Hardly ever. They still didn't. But Frankie insisted 'they' weren't working anymore. That she needed space. Needed time.

He'd made the monumental mistake of asking her if she was going through some kind of mid-life crisis. Although weren't they kind of past mid-life in their early sixties? Or was that the new mid-life these days?

Frankie had stalked out of the room when he asked that. He'd never been one to discuss feelings or emotions, but he'd been trying these last few months. Really trying. But nothing was working.

He suggested a therapist, but Frankie said it was something she had to work out on her own. He suggested date nights. He came home precisely at dinnertime instead of whatever late hour he used to come home. But Frankie no longer made them dinner. Didn't want date nights. Didn't really want anything from him.

Well, she had asked him for one thing.

She asked him to move out of the house.

He slammed his suitcase shut and tossed it to the floor. It rolled away on its four wheels, and he glared at it. Everything wanted to get away from him.

He grabbed his keys and wallet from the dresser and hauled the suitcase out to the garage, where he shoved it into the trunk of his car. He debated going back upstairs to get Frankie's suitcase, but would she take that wrong? These days, he was afraid to ask her things or suggest things or even breathe the same air as Frankie.

He'd made so many mistakes. So many. He'd give anything to go back a few years. Okay, more than a few. Throw himself one hundred percent into their marriage. Show her how he felt about her. Because he did love her. They'd just drifted apart. Way apart. And Frankie wanted it even further apart. She wanted him out.

There were some nice new condos near his work, but he didn't really want to live in a condo. Maybe he could find a suitable little house somewhere nearby. But what did he need with a whole house when it was just him?

He headed back inside and found Frankie in the kitchen, suitcase by her side. Her slacks and pale yellow blouse were precisely ironed, and a light sweater tied gracefully around her shoulders completed the smart look. These days she complained about the extra pounds that had settled on her hips and her rounded stomach, but he thought she looked smashing. Sexy in that way women could get as they aged and blossomed into their maturity.

"Can I get that for you?" he asked tentatively, looking toward the luggage.

She nodded, then followed him out to the garage after he grabbed it.

While he situated her suitcase in the trunk with his identical one—they were a perfectly matched pair—she slipped into the car without a word. He hurried to the driver's side and then pulled the car out of the garage. The garage door lumbered down, and he couldn't help but think it was closing on a part of his life he would never get back.

"You have your phone?" she asked.

"Yes."

He was partially surprised she hadn't come in and questioned his packing. She was always reminding him to put in his swimsuit when they vacationed or asking if he was sure he had enough clean shirts. But this time she'd been silent. And he wasn't sure if he *had* put in enough shirts.

He glanced over at her as he drove them down the highway, her profile a stony mask of indifference. Or maybe annoyance. An hour's drive or so. Maybe without saying a word to each other?

Well, this trip hadn't been his plan. A year ago, maybe he might have thought of planning a nice trip for their anniversary. Oh, who was he kidding? He wouldn't have thought of it. He would have been lucky if he remembered the anniversary at all and that it was a big one. Leave it to Katie to remember the anniversary and insist they all take a vacation with a week-long celebration.

Seven days. He could do this. Couldn't he?

CHAPTER 2

The silence settled between them like an icy glacier. Frankie wasn't certain how she felt about going back to the resort after all these years. To where they'd honeymooned. It was Murphy's resort back then, but the girls said it had recently been purchased and remodeled. Which was good, because it hadn't been the nicest back then, but it had been all they could afford for their three-night honeymoon.

She carefully faced straight ahead, watching the white lines slip past them. Will finally turned on the radio to a station playing the oldies classics she liked instead of the country music he preferred. She probably should thank him.

But still, they rode on in silence. Her jaw

muscles screamed at her from clenching her teeth. She glanced down at her fist resting in her lap and slowly uncurled her fingers. Will looked unaffected by their silence, by the tension. He almost looked… relaxed. But then he'd always loved a road trip.

Will finally pulled the car into the resort and she glanced around. Okay, this was very different from before. The cottages were brightly painted and the courtyard had been planted with flowering bushes. Comfortable chairs were scattered around the area. Each porch had chairs beckoning the guests. And not the rusty metals ones that had been here before. Of course, it had been forty years, she reminded herself. A lot can change in forty years. A lot. She cringed at the irony of her words.

"It looks different, doesn't it?" Will's words broke through her thoughts.

"Yes. It does."

"It was kind of a dive before." He let out a soft chortle. "But I thought it was extravagant back then to spend three days right on the water. Had to work that extra night job to afford the wedding and honeymoon."

She remembered. He had worked hard to

give her a nice wedding. Just the two of them married at a small church in the country. She'd sewn her own wedding dress and thought it was lovely at the time. Though looking back at the few photos they had, she winced at its fit. It had been the style of dress at the time, but it wasn't a good style for her. She'd been rail thin back then. Not carrying the extra pounds she did now with the bit of a stomach pouch.

Pushing away her thoughts of her current weight, she went back to her memories of their wedding. Will had worn a new suit and looked totally ill at ease. He'd gotten her a bouquet of lilacs, her favorite flowers.

"And it took us like ten hours to drive here to Moonbeam from northern Georgia. We drove all night after the wedding ceremony. I was so tired when we got here." His lips tilted in a lazy smile.

"We got here early morning and took a beach walk, still in our wedding clothes." The waves had splashed the bottom of her dress, but they laughed and raced down the beach. So happy. So in love. So… young.

Will turned off the engine. "We did get here early. Took that walk. Then we went and got breakfast in town, and Murphy let us check in early to our cottage."

All those memories came rushing back to her. She'd been so nervous, but Will had been so gentle and understanding. She'd thought she was the luckiest girl in the world.

And how did they get from that day to this one? She didn't think Will even liked her very much anymore, much less loved her. She'd been invisible for years.

He opened his car door. "Let's go get checked in."

She sucked in a deep breath of the salty air and climbed out of the car. She could do this. It was only one week.

CHAPTER 3

V iolet stood on the front porch of the office of Blue Heron Cottages sweeping the weathered boards. She paused, looking across the courtyard. Did that bougainvillea bush need trimming? Was it the right time to trim it back some? She'd never lived in Florida before buying the resort, and there were so many plants she wasn't familiar with. But she loved them all. The pretty pink blossoms on the bougainvillea. The scent of the gardenias. And the palm trees. She loved all the palm trees scattered around the property. A lovely live oak stretched its branches out, welcoming their guests and providing shade for sitting on the bright wooden bench she'd placed under it.

A car pulled up, and she leaned the broom against the wall. A couple got out and headed toward her. She smiled at them. "Welcome to Blue Heron Cottages."

"Good afternoon," the man said as he climbed the stairs and glanced back at the woman. "We're the Winters. We have a reservation for a week."

"Come in. I'll get you all registered."

They followed her inside, and she glanced at the computer. "Ah, yes. Here you are. And I see your daughters—right? I think that's what Ms. Winters said when she made the reservations. They're right next door."

"Yes, our daughters Katie and Stacey," Mrs. Winters said.

"I hope you have a wonderful family vacation." Violet handed them their door keys. "You're in the yellow cottage, and your daughters are next door in the mint green one."

Mr. Winters reached out and took the keys. "Are the girls here yet?"

"No, not yet."

He nodded. "I'm sure they'll be here soon. We all live just out of Sarasota. It's about an hour's drive and they decided to drive down separately from us."

"When they check in, I'll let them know you're here."

The couple walked out of the office, Mrs. Winters taking the lead and Mr. Winters trailing behind her. They'd kept their distance from each other in the office, too. An awkward vibe hovered around them. Or maybe she was just imagining that. But she was usually a great judge of people. And they looked like a couple who didn't want to be in the same room with each other.

Well, none of her business. Okay, it was some of her business because the daughters had planned a surprise anniversary celebration in the courtyard. A guest list of about twenty-five people. Friends driving in from Sarasota on Saturday afternoon for the party. Mr. and Mrs. Winters thought they were just going out to dinner for their anniversary with the girls. But their daughter Katie had planned the courtyard celebration.

Personally, Violet hated surprises. But hopefully their daughters knew what they were doing.

She headed back out to the porch and grabbed the broom, hoping to get the chore finished before any more guests arrived.

CHAPTER 4

K atie drove her new Tesla to the resort. Stacey made fun of the car and teased her about how expensive it was. And mentioned how inconvenient it was to find places to charge it. But she'd looked it up and there was a charging station—two, actually—at a service station just outside of town on the interstate. She rarely treated herself to anything extravagant, but she'd gotten a big promotion and jump in pay and decided she was worth it. She loved everything about the car. All the technology in it. Everything. But then, she'd always been a techie person. The person her parents and Stacey called if anything went wrong with their laptops, televisions, or phones.

And as much teasing as Stacey did, she didn't complain about Katie doing the driving and paying for the charging of the car. For that matter, so far Katie had paid for everything for their parents' anniversary celebration, too. Surely Stacey was going to offer to contribute some amount of money. Maybe. She still hadn't paid her half of last year's Christmas present or Mom's birthday present. They always gave a present from both of them, but Katie ended up coming up with an idea, getting the gifts, and paying for them. Stacey was *super* good at adding her name to the cards, though…

Stacey glanced at the big screen on the dash. "Looks like we're almost there."

"Almost." She loved the big screen on her Tesla, with all the information it provided. It made her feel in control. She swatted her sister's hand away as Stacey reached to mess with the display. "Did you think Mom and Dad acted a bit strange when we told them we booked this vacation for all of us?"

Stacey shook her head. "Strange? No, I think they were just surprised."

"They're going to be more surprised when

they find out we planned a whole vow renewal ceremony for them and invited some of their friends down."

"Oh, they'll love it. I mean, who wouldn't?"

Katie frowned. Would they love it? She'd gotten pretty carried away with the planning. But it had been so much fun. She'd ordered food for a small reception from Sea Glass Cafe. Hired a photographer to take photos since her parents had never had real photos of their wedding, just a few quick shots taken with a Polaroid. The owner of the resort, Violet, had helped her with some of the plans.

"You think Mom ever went and bought a dress?" Stacey asked.

"Not last I talked to her." That annoyed her, too. Why hadn't her mother gotten a dress? A forty-year anniversary was a big deal. That was a lot of years. It was special.

She, herself, had gone out and bought a new dress to wear. Two, actually. She wasn't certain which one she wanted to wear, so she brought them both with her.

They drove down the main street in town. Stacey pointed. "Hey, there's a dress shop.

Barbara's Boutique. Maybe we could take Mom shopping there."

"That's a great idea." Nice of Stacey to come up with one idea since she'd been not so helpful with this whole celebration. Katie had gotten invitations printed and mailed out with a note that it was a surprise, so not to mention it to her folks. About twenty of her parents' closest friends were going to drive down on Saturday. Luckily, the resort was fairly close to home.

"I bet we can talk Mom into going shopping." Stacey looked pleased with herself for coming up with the idea.

Katie pointed out the window. "There's the floral shop Violet had me talk to. The owner, Daisy, was really helpful. We're going to have bouquets on the serving table and some flowers on the arbor." She'd also made up a playlist of songs and brought two decent speakers so they could play music for the reception.

Stacey hadn't volunteered to help with anything. Well, she'd said to let her know if there was anything she could do. But she hadn't actually jumped in to do anything. That was par for the course for Stacey, though. She liked others to take charge.

Anyway, almost everything was ready. She wanted to pop into the flower shop and talk to Daisy in person. And she talked to an Evelyn at Sea Glass Cafe and would go there and meet her in person to make certain everything was just right with the food order.

"Here it is," Stacey said as they pulled up. A new-looking sign proclaimed Blue Heron Cottages.

"I think it's cool we're having it at the same place Mom and Dad went for their honeymoon." She looked at the pretty cottages scattered around. It looked perfect. All her hard work was going to pay off. She just knew it. "Come on. Let's check in." She slid out of the car and bounded up the steps. She turned back. "You coming?"

"You check us in. I've got a phone call to make."

Katie shook her head. *Sure, I'll check us in. No problem.* Put the room on her credit card. Maybe she could cart in Stacey's luggage for her, too. Sometimes her little sister annoyed her to no end.

Frankie followed Will into the yellow cottage. Light streamed through the windows, cheerful beach prints hung on the wall, and a painted table and chairs sat in the corner.

"This doesn't look anything like when we were here on our honeymoon." Will turned around and set down their suitcases.

"No, it's very nice." Way nicer than before. She took a few steps down the hallway and was pleased to see there were two bedrooms. "I'll take the bedroom on the left."

Will came up behind her and set her suitcase in the room. "Looks like we'll have to share the bathroom, though."

She nodded. "Let's keep the bedroom doors closed in case the girls come in. So they won't… know."

"Sure." He pivoted and left her room.

Rustling noises came from the room across the hall. This small cottage was getting tinier by the minute, sucking away her breath. She wanted to race outside and take a walk on the beach, but she should unpack first. Make sure her things didn't wrinkle.

She methodically hung up her dresses and tops. Put some shorts and two swimsuits in the drawer. She grabbed her toiletries and went to put them in the bathroom.

Will came walking out of it. "I just have my Dopp kit. Won't take up much room."

She hung her hanging bag of toiletries on the back of the door and walked back into her room. She stood there and looked around. Is this what it would be like? Just staying in this one room the whole week to avoid Will?

"Hey, Frankie, the girls are here," Will called out.

She took a deep breath. The girls would be a good buffer. It was all going to be okay. She stepped out of her room and closed her door. Will had left his bedroom door open even though she'd asked him to keep it closed. She took two quick steps over and jerked the door shut. She didn't ask much of him. He could at least keep the door closed so they didn't get questions from the girls.

She twirled around and headed out to the main room of the cottage. Katie stood in the room by Will, and Stacey stood in the doorway. "Stacey, come in and close the door. You're letting out all the cool air."

"Nice to see you, Mom." Stacey rolled her

eyes, stepped inside, and closed the door behind her.

"Did you girls have a nice drive?" She ignored Stacey's eye roll. Wasn't she a little too old to be rolling her eyes at her mother? Didn't kids outgrow that sometime in high school?

"It was nice." Katie walked over and hugged her.

"Her car is like riding in a computer. It practically drives itself." Stacey plopped down on an overstuffed chair.

Katie glared at her sister. So far, this wasn't turning out great.

"So, do you girls want to go take a walk on the beach with me?"

"I still need to unpack," Katie said. "Don't want things to get wrinkled."

Stacey jumped back up. "I'll walk. I don't care if my stuff gets wrinkled. Dad, you coming?"

"I, uh…" Will looked at her and she nodded.

"You should come. You love a good beach walk," she added.

"Sure, sounds like a plan. Katydid, why

don't you come with us? It will be fun." Will grinned at Katie. "You know you want to go."

Katie laughed. "Like I can ever say no to you when you call me Katydid. Sure, why not? I can always iron things later."

They all headed out into the sunshine. Her family. Will and the girls. But it was strange and a bit strained, like she was just going through the motions. She lagged behind the others, watching them laugh and hip-check each other, and Katie stopped to pick up a shell. Of course. Katie loved to go shelling. So did she, for that matter. Maybe she'd find time to sneak away by herself and get a good shell-seeking expedition in. Besides, it would be time outside, away from Will. Then she'd be able to relax.

A light breeze blew her hair around her face, and she wished she'd clipped it back. She reached up and tucked it behind her ears.

"Come on, Mom. Catch up." Katie turned and waved to her.

She picked up her pace and met them at the water's edge, letting the waves lap over her feet. The water was warm, and the sun sparkled on the waves. She took a deep breath of the salty air and tried to relax. They could all have a good time this week. She wanted the week to go well. Very well.

Because she knew it was the last family vacation they'd ever take.

CHAPTER 5

Frankie tugged on shorts and a t-shirt and slipped out of the cottage early the next morning to go for a long walk on the beach. She'd heard Will stirring in the room across the hall and wanted to give him time alone to get up and get ready. And avoid him. When she got back, hopefully he'd go somewhere and she could shower and get ready for the day.

The sun was just tossing soft pink colors into the sky. No breeze stirred the palm trees this morning, and the waves gently lapped the shore in a slow, undulating motion. She headed up the beach, enjoying being alone with no stress of hiding the truth from the girls or dealing with Will.

She knew he was frustrated with her. That much was obvious. But then, she'd spent years being frustrated with him. He hardly noticed her. They didn't talk about anything since the girls moved out. Oh, they might talk about the weather, or a home repair, or if a car needed work. Nothing that really mattered. He didn't ask about her day, but then, she no longer asked him how work was, either.

At least when the girls had been home, they talked about the girls. But everything changed when they became empty nesters. And Will got a promotion and worked insane hours with lots of trips out of town.

She'd struggled, alone in the house. It had been such a change. The girls didn't need her anymore. Will was barely home. She took up yoga and bought a treadmill, but even that didn't keep the weight off. She took a painting class and learned to knit. Well, kind of learned to knit. Nothing fancy. But she'd knitted a few scarves.

But she felt invisible to Will. Invisible to everyone.

She'd tried yet another part-time job—two, actually—but they didn't work out. But then she didn't have much experience doing anything that was valued much for a job.

Maybe she could sort everything out when Will moved out of the house and she didn't have the daily stress of living with him. It figured his work travel would cut back right when she needed space. Needed time to figure out who she was now. The girls didn't need her. Will never looked at her like he even saw her. When was the last time he'd kissed her? She couldn't even remember, but it was probably a peck on the cheek sometime when he was leaving on one of his many business trips.

And Will. How did she feel about him? He'd gotten more handsome as he aged, in that aggravating way men did. He'd matured with slightly graying hair and smile wrinkles around his chestnut-brown eyes. His hair was still thick with slight waves, unlike her thinning hair. He still had a trim waist, strong shoulders, and an all-year tan from working out in the yard or playing golf.

She glanced down at her thickening waist. No matter what she did. Exercise. Sit-ups. Her waist still was inches thicker than it used to be. Her face was fuller now, too. Her hair was mostly gray. And her wrinkles didn't look like smile lines. They looked like… wrinkles. No wonder Will didn't look at her the way he used to. She looked old. Tired.

She thrust the critical, confusing thoughts from her mind, reminding herself she was out here to relax. She walked along the edge of the water, letting the waves lap at her feet. A small shell, laced with purple along its edges, called to her and she leaned down to pick it up, admiring it. So pretty. She rinsed it in the water and dropped it into her pocket.

As she got back near the cottages, she spotted an older woman sitting on the beach. Well, not a lot older. She kept forgetting she herself was in her sixties.

The woman looked up, smiled, and waved. "Good morning. Gorgeous morning for a walk."

She headed toward the woman. "It really is. I'd forgotten how much I love a good beach walk."

"You staying at the cottages?"

"I am."

"I'm staying here, too. I've been here for a bit. I keep extending my stay. I'm Rose." She reached out her hand.

Frankie took her hand and smiled. "I'm Francine. Everyone calls me Frankie."

"Nice to meet you, Frankie. You here alone?"

"No, I'm with my husband. And our daughters are staying in the cottage next to us."

"Oh, a family vacation. How nice."

"It's actually a surprise trip the girls planned for us."

"That was nice of them."

"It was. It's… it's our fortieth anniversary, and they wanted to do something special for it. We're going out to dinner on Saturday, our actual anniversary."

"That sounds wonderful. Forty years. Quite an accomplishment these days. Happy anniversary."

And what did she say to that? Thank you, but it might be our last one? My husband is moving out as soon as we get home?

"I was married to my Emmett for almost fifty years. He's passed now."

"I'm sorry."

Rose's lips rose in a gentle smile. "I miss him every day. Well, you must understand that. I'm sure you'd miss your husband too, after forty years."

There was no proper answer to that. Well, nothing she could share with Rose. So she just smiled at her. Again.

"It was nice chatting with you. Have a wonderful stay here at the cottages. They really are nice. My Emmett and I used to come here every year. They were... let's just say a bit more run down then."

Frankie laughed. "We actually honeymooned here. The cottages were so plain then. In need of repair. But we thought it was so extravagant to stay in a cottage right on the beach."

"Violet has done a wonderful job with remodeling the resort. It's so cheerful and pretty now."

"It really is. Well, I should probably head back. See if the girls are up." She turned and headed back to the yellow cottage. Will was sitting out on the porch, drinking coffee.

"Morning. I made a whole pot. There's plenty for you." Will tilted his head toward the door.

"Thanks, I'll grab a cup and then jump in

the shower," she said, hoping he got the hint to stay outside while she got ready.

"Sounds good." He leaned back in his chair and stretched out his legs as if he didn't have a care in the world.

And that annoyed her.

She went inside and shut the door firmly behind her. Why was she so stressed and upset and he acted like everything was just fine?

CHAPTER 6

Melody walked over to Blue Heron Cottages. Restless energy flowed through her, and even the brisk walk didn't seem to take the edge off of it.

Violet sat on the office porch with Rose, sipping coffee. Melody walked past the blooming hibiscus bushes and up to the porch. Violet jumped up. "Hey there. Didn't expect to see you until Friday at happy hour. You and Ethan are still coming, aren't you? Let me get you some coffee."

"We are. I mean, I guess we are." You know, if tomorrow didn't blow up in her face and she and Ethan were no longer friends. She climbed the steps and sank onto a comfortable chair—

painted a bright peach color, of course. Violet painted everything a bright color. "And yes, to the coffee."

Violet disappeared into the office.

"Hey, Rose." She briefly wondered if Rose was ever going to leave the cottages. The woman had checked in weeks ago, then kept extending her stay. Though everyone adored Rose and loved that she stayed on.

"Morning, Melody. Glad you decided to join us for coffee."

"I just needed to… I don't know. Get out and walk a bit."

"What gives?" Violet came back out, handed her a cup of coffee, and sat in the chair beside her. "You look kind of…" Violet frowned. "Kind of upset?"

"Nerves. It's nerves."

"Nerves? What are you nervous about?"

Melody leaned back in her chair. "So, you know how I told you Ethan finally asked me out? And that after deliberating for days, I said yes, I would go out with him?"

"Right, you told me."

"Well, he wants to go out *tomorrow* night. Tomorrow. Out to eat."

"And you said yes, right?" Violet's eyebrows creased.

"Yes, I agreed to it." Melody drummed her fingers on the arm of her chair. "But now I'm second-guessing myself. Do you know how many years it's been since I've gone out with someone?"

"A long time, I'm guessing."

"Very long time. I'm not sure I even know how to act. What to wear. I'm ridiculously nervous, which is silly because it's Ethan. He's easy to be with. Fun. Easy to talk to. But what if going out with him messes all that up? It seems so strange to go out with someone besides John. And I miss John."

Rose reached over and took her hand. "I know you miss John. It must be hard to move on. But going out with Ethan doesn't erase the wonderful life you had with John."

"I just feel a bit guilty. Like I'm... I'm cheating on John or something."

Rose gave her a gentle smile. "I bet John would want you to be happy."

She sighed. "I know he would. It just all seems so confusing right now."

Violet shook her head. "Are you trying to

talk yourself out of it? Because I think Ethan is great. You'll have a wonderful time if you just relax."

"I guess so. Maybe." Melody shrugged. "It was easier when I thought we were just friends."

"You're still friends. You're just going on a date. And really, it's been clear to everyone— except you—that Ethan is crazy about you." Violet took a sip of her coffee.

"You think?"

"I know."

"What do you think I should wear? I feel like all my outfits are suitable for work at the cafe, not for going out."

"Surely you have a cute dress you could wear." Rose leaned forward in her chair. "I bet you do."

"I'd have to dig in the back of my closet to find one. If they even fit anymore. I've put on a few pounds since working at the cafe. Too much pie." Melody shrugged. "Who knew dating could be this complicated?"

"You could go buy a new dress," Violet suggested.

"Maybe."

"Tell you what. I'll go with you to Barbara's

Boutique when it opens. We'll look for an outfit." Violet set her cup down, her eyes shining with enthusiasm.

"Really? That might be nice." It might be fun to have something new to wear. Something Ethan hadn't seen her in twenty times before. Maybe it would make her feel more comfortable about this whole date thing. Less nervous.

"Perfect. It's a plan. I'll meet you there at ten this morning. That will give me some time to finish up a few things here at the cottages."

Getting a nice new dress was good, but it did little to allay her fears. She ran her finger around the rim of the coffee cup. "But what if this whole dating Ethan blows up on me? What if…" And *this* is what she constantly worried about. "What if he wants to kiss me good night when he drops me off?"

Rose chuckled. "Let's not borrow trouble. What if you have a fabulous time? What if he *does* kiss you and that's fabulous, too?"

Melody took the last sip of her coffee and stood, exasperated with herself. "I'm driving myself crazy thinking about everything."

"You should just relax and enjoy yourself. Try to quit worrying," Rose said.

"Easier said than done. Thanks for letting me talk things out with you guys. Not that I feel any better. But at least I have a plan for what to wear." Melody grinned. "You're both good friends."

"Glad to help. And we'll find the perfect dress. I promise." Violet stood. "I should get back to work. See you at ten."

Rose pushed out of her chair. "I should go, too. I have a new book waiting for me at Beachside Bookshop. I think I'll wander over that way and pick it up."

Melody climbed down the stairs and walked across the crushed shell walkway. She hoped Violet and Rose were right. That everything would be okay. But at this point, she just wanted the date to be over and behind her. Ugh. Why had she said yes?

Melody swore Violet had her try on two dozen dresses—maybe three dozen. Violet made a no pile, a maybe pile, and a yes pile.

"This one?" Melody spun around in front of the mirror in a pretty light teal dress with cap sleeves. It hit about her knees—her preferred length. It did fit her perfectly.

"That's my favorite. For sure. But I think you should also get the yellow one. Because I bet he asks you out again soon. And while you're at it, that navy-striped one was adorable."

"I don't need three dresses."

"Oh, go on. All three look wonderful on you. And if you don't get them now, you'll just be back shopping again soon." Violet laughed. "Now, how about some fun tops to wear, too?"

"That's not a bad idea," she reluctantly agreed. "I could use something besides Sea Glass Cafe tops."

Violet jumped up and went over to a rack of tops and picked out a handful. "Here, try these on. See if you like them."

They finally agreed on four new tops and she paid for the clothing. "Thanks, Margaret. You have the best clothes here."

"Thank you, dear."

"You sure have an eye for ordering in just the right things," Violet said. "Love shopping here."

"Thank you. You two have a good day." Margaret handed her the packages.

They walked outside into the sunshine. "I should probably go drop these off at home. Then I have a shift at the cafe. Then, of course, my... date... tomorrow." It still sounded strange to say she had a date.

"I bet you have a wonderful time." Violet hugged her. "You need to relax, quit overthinking, and just enjoy yourself."

Melody laughed. "You know me so well."

"I know you well enough to know you're going to fret all day. And tomorrow. At least you have a shift at the cafe to keep you busy."

"And I'm working breakfast and lunch tomorrow. I hope we have a ton of customers and I don't have a minute to think."

"After this first date, the next one will be easier."

"You think we'll have *another* date?"

Violet grinned. "I think you'll have a lot of them." She turned and headed down the sidewalk with a quick wave of her hand.

Melody headed back to her house, a bag in each hand. She couldn't believe Violet had talked her into buying so many new things. But then, she couldn't remember the last time she'd been shopping for clothes. It was kind of nice to think about having new clothes to wear. And she loved the teal dress. It would be perfect for tomorrow. Not too fancy. Just perfect.

Now, if she could just get through today and tomorrow without changing her mind and calling Ethan to cancel.

CHAPTER 7

Katie sat on a chair in the cottage she was sharing with Stacey. She'd been up for hours, sipping strong black coffee. Stacey had never been an early riser and today was no exception. She finally heard the shower running, and soon Stacey came out, her damp hair hanging around her shoulders. She wore a very old, faded t-shirt and shorts. The kind of outfit Katie would have only worn in her own home.

Oblivious to Katie's silent criticism, Stacey walked over to the coffeepot and poured a cup. "We should have picked up cream last night. I like cream in my coffee."

"I'll pick some up today." She scribbled cream on the list she'd been making.

Stacey walked over and sank into a chair by the window. "What time did you get up?"

"Hours ago."

"But you're on vacation. You should sleep in."

She didn't even answer her sister.

Stacey took a sip of her coffee, made a face, and set the cup down on the table beside her. "Dinner was nice last night, wasn't it?"

Katie frowned. "Did you think Mom and Dad were acting funny when we went on that walk yesterday? And then at dinner, they sat on opposite sides of the table so I sat by Dad and you by Mom. What was up with that?"

"I don't know." Stacey shrugged. "They seemed fine to me."

Her parents had seemed a bit odd yesterday. She was sure of it. Dad usually teased Mom and made her laugh. There was none of that. Mom had been unusually quiet. Not even bombarding them with questions about what they'd been up to like she usually did. "Well, I think something is wrong. Wondering if they're having a fight or something."

"They never fight." Stacey shook her head,

took another sip, and frowned into the cup as if she could make cream appear.

"That we know of," Katie added.

"Maybe they were just tired."

But her mom hadn't looked tired as much as… what was that expression she'd had? Maybe sad? But why would she be sad? They were on a family vacation. Mom loved when all of them could be together. She was celebrating forty years with Dad. There was just no reason to be sad. She'd watch her mother today. See how she was.

Her sister had a way of ignoring things, oblivious to others' problems. Skipping through life without a care. Always thinking of herself. As opposed to the way Katie thought, always worrying about others and how they were doing. She often wondered how her parents could have two daughters who were so very different. Stacey lived paycheck to paycheck, often changing jobs. Never saving.

That would drive her crazy. She saved money from each paycheck. Budgeted for expenses. Contributed to her IRA with every single check. She'd been with the same company for years. She loved the stability it gave her life.

"So, what's on the agenda today?" Stacey asked, unaware of her sister's critical thoughts.

"I want to go to the florist. Check on the arrangements."

"You don't need me for that, do you? I think I'm going to go to the beach. Get some sun."

"Sure, that's fine." What had she expected? That her sister would jump in and help with the last of the details for the party?

"I'll text Mom and Dad and see if they want to go to the beach. I'll just say you had to run to town to get something. You can join us when you get back."

"Sure, sounds like a plan." She stood and grabbed her list and her purse. "I'll be back in a while."

She gritted her teeth and stalked out of the cottage, reminding herself not to slam the door behind her. Her sister could be so exasperating. So unhelpful. So... Stacey.

Well, she'd just finalize all the details herself. Because she wanted the celebration to be perfect. Wanted to do that for her parents. Okay, and she wanted it to be perfect because she didn't want problems to arise. She wanted everyone to have a wonderful time.

She slipped into the Tesla and sighed. The car always made her feel good. It's sleekness. The technology. The fact that she bought it with money she'd saved by carefully budgeting.

She pulled out of the drive and headed into town, driving along Magnolia until she found the floral shop. She parked in front of it and got out. Such a cute, quaint little town. The kind that should be in a sweet holiday movie where a woman returns after years away and falls back in love with her high school sweetheart. Or something like that. She shook her head at her crazy thoughts and walked into the floral shop, Beach Blooms.

"Good morning." A woman stood behind the counter arranging yellow roses in a pretty crystal vase.

"Hi. I'm Katie Winters. I talked to you about flowers for the anniversary party for my parents."

"Oh, yes. I'm Daisy. I have the flowers ordered. Do you want to pick them up Saturday morning, or should I deliver them?"

"I guess deliver them?" And it occurred to

her that it would be hard to hide the whole surprise from her parents if the courtyard was being all set up. Though, maybe they would think it was for some event for someone else. She'd have to figure that all out.

"I got the hydrangeas you wanted. And you wanted a bouquet for your mom, right?"

"Right. I'm not sure what flowers to get for that. Do you have a suggestion? Something simple."

"Well, I'm always a fan of daisies." Daisy grinned. "And some baby's breath and some greenery. Or roses are always a good choice."

"Let's go with white flowers. Roses and whatever you think would look good with them. And not a really large bouquet. Smaller." Her mother wouldn't want a large bouquet, would she?

"Perfect. And you said this was a surprise for them, right?"

"Yes, they don't know anything about it."

"We'll see if we can make it perfect for them."

"That's what I'm hoping for." She left Beach Blooms feeling better after meeting Daisy in person and seeing the beautiful arrangements in the shop. She was certain Daisy would do a great job with the flowers.

She stopped and picked up cream for Stacey —because she couldn't tolerate another morning of her heavy sighs about her coffee— and headed back to the cottages.

Frankie stretched out on the lounge chair under the umbrella. "You want some sunscreen?" she asked Stacey after carefully applying it to every inch of her skin even though she was under the umbrella.

"Nah, I'm good." Stacey had pulled her chair out into the sun.

"You really should wear sunscreen, you know."

"Maybe in a bit." Annoyance tinged her words.

Frankie sighed and slipped the sunscreen into her beach bag. Stacey never did like to be told to do anything. But sunscreen was important. She took the sunscreen back out of her bag and placed it close to Stacey. Maybe she'd take the hint and put it on in a bit.

Katie came walking up to them and sank onto the chair next to her, out of the direct sun. "Where's Dad?" she asked as she took a book out of her bag, then a towel.

"He said he had errands to run in town." Though she wasn't sure what kind of errands he needed to do, but maybe he was just giving her space like she'd asked. Anyway, this way she could enjoy some beach time with her daughters. It would be easier to hide the truth from them if Will wasn't around stressing her out.

Katie took out some lotion and started to apply it. Frankie smothered a self-satisfied smile. Ha, at least one daughter had listened to her and knew the benefits of sun protection.

"He's not much on just sitting around, is he?" Stacey asked. "Bet when he gets back he goes for a walk or something."

"Maybe we could all play croquet later today. I saw there was a set in the courtyard." Katie suggested.

"That might be nice." Frankie couldn't think

of a way to say no. She realized she was going to have to spend time doing things with Will this week. And really, she wanted to enjoy this time with her family, she did. She turned to Stacey. "So, how's your new job going?"

"It's okay. Not sure I'll stay there, though. It's not quite what I expected."

"Make sure you stay until you find something new." She couldn't quite stop herself from giving advice and was fairly certain Stacey rolled her eyes behind her sunglasses.

"I thought you said this was going to be the perfect job." Katie stretched out on the lounge chair.

"My boss is pretty demanding. And they weren't crazy about giving me the week off since I just started a couple of weeks ago. But I told them going in that I needed the week off."

"How's your job, Katie?" She turned to her other daughter.

"Great. You know I got that promotion not long ago and there's a chance I might be up for another one the beginning of next year."

"That's wonderful, honey."

"How about you, Mom? Take up anything

fun recently?" Katie took a bottle of water out of her bag. "Want one?"

"Yes, thank you." Leave it to Katie to be so organized that she brought water for them. "No new crafts or hobbies. Still working on my knitting but not getting much better. Enjoying it though. I'm thinking of looking for another part-time job."

"Dad still traveling so much?" Katie asked.

"Ah, no. Not as much." Which was too bad. Because the stress in the house when he was home was unbearable. But this was nice. Being here on the beach. Chatting with the girls. Relaxing. So nice. She didn't have to worry about Will or find a way to avoid him.

The breeze had picked up from this morning and ruffled her hair. It was actually pleasant sitting here under the bright umbrella. Each umbrella on the beach—provided by Violet—was a different bright shade with colorful chairs beneath them. So different than when she and Will had honeymooned here. No nice lounge chairs then. No umbrellas.

She pushed her thoughts away from their honeymoon. Hadn't she just been enjoying time with her girls without Will being around? She didn't need to be thinking about him now.

"I thought we'd go to Jimmy's on the Wharf for dinner tonight. Violet said it was really good. And I'd love to see the wharf. How does that sound?" Katie glanced over at her.

"It sounds lovely." Though that would just be one more time they'd have to hide what was happening from the girls. It was already getting hard to do. Last night at dinner she'd struggled to relax and act like she was having a good time. She'd have to do better with it tonight, or Katie was sure to pick up on it. Know something was wrong. She doubted if Stacey would pick up on anything though. Her youngest was pretty oblivious to others. A charming girl—okay, woman now—but a bit self-absorbed. Stacey had on a shockingly tiny bikini while Katie wore a modest two-piece.

She looked down at her sensible one-piece swimsuit. Navy blue stripes. Her old swimsuits didn't fit her any longer, and she'd gotten this new one earlier this summer. In a size that made her cringe. And it even had tummy control in it, so the tag had said. Though, she wasn't sure she'd call her tummy controlled. It was still pudgy.

"Hey, Mom. Stacey and I were talking. How about tomorrow we go into town and go shopping? Maybe we'll find you a new dress to wear for your anniversary."

"Oh, I don't need a new one."

"Well, let's go shopping, and maybe Stacey or I will find something we like."

She nodded, fully aware that Katie would badger her into getting a new dress. "Sure, shopping sounds good."

Katie smiled, obviously pleased she'd agreed to the shopping trip. Katie probably had the whole week planned out. Her oldest daughter was a planner, an organizer. Stacey was more of a go-with-the-flow type person. It was like she just let life happen to her while Katie planned every step of her life. But they both seemed happy, and that's what really mattered.

"I'll go shopping if Mom's buying." Stacey grinned.

Of course she'd be buying. She always did when the three of them went shopping. And they hadn't gone shopping in a long time. It would be fun. She loved spoiling them. And Will wouldn't go shopping with them, so they'd have a day of just girl time. Maybe they'd even have a girls' lunch. Tomorrow was looking brighter and brighter.

She leaned back in the chair, relaxed, and savored these moments alone with her girls.

CHAPTER 8

W ill drove into town, giving Frankie time alone with the girls. Besides, it had been so tense at dinner last night. He wasn't ready to go through that again. He'd been hoping maybe, just maybe, this time with the family would show Frankie what she'd be missing if they separated. Or worse... if she wanted to make the separation... permanent. But he couldn't bear to even think about that. Surely it wouldn't come to that. Frankie would just take some time to sort things out and everything would go back to normal.

Only he wasn't so sure of that. He wasn't sure of anything anymore. He pulled his car into a parking spot on Magnolia and sat, staring out the window. How had it come to this? Oh, he knew part of it was his fault. Most of it. It was. He should have given their marriage more attention. Spent more time with her. He'd just been so busy with his job. But was that really an excuse? Didn't everyone make time for things that were truly important to them?

He'd tried to do better this last year, but Frankie was so distant. Nothing he did seemed to get through to her. Nothing changed her attitude now that she wanted him out of the house. It was like he'd missed his chance to fix things. And the thing was, he couldn't really blame her. He had been busy and didn't appreciate her and rarely made time to spend with her. Boy, did he regret all that now.

He sighed and slowly climbed out of the car. What to do to kill a few hours? He glanced along the street, looking at all the signs. Maybe he'd do some browsing at the bookshop. Or go grab some coffee at the Sea Glass Cafe he saw down the way. Then he spied a florist, and he came up with an idea.

He hurried down the street and entered the

shop. The fragrance of all the flowers surrounded him, mocking him, reminding him how long it had been since he'd been in a flower shop. How long *had* it been since he'd bought Frankie flowers?

A very long time.

"Hi, welcome to Beach Blooms. I'm Daisy." A woman behind the counter greeted him.

Great name for a florist. He smiled at her. "Hi... I was wondering. It's my anniversary on Saturday and I thought that I would like to get my wife a bouquet of lilacs."

"They're out of season now and don't grow in Florida, but I could try to source some for you."

"She loves them. I'd like to surprise her with them."

"Okay, let me see what I can do. They might be kind of pricey."

"I don't care what it would cost."

"Okay, give me your name and information and I'll see what I can do."

"Will Winters. I'm in town staying at Blue Heron Cottages."

Her eyebrows rose slightly, then she jotted

his name on her order pad. "Ah, okay, Mr. Winters. If you give me your cell phone number, I'll call and let you know if I can find some for you."

"That would be perfect. Now I just need to find a small gift for her. She said no gifts, but I still would like to find her a little something."

"Good luck with that. There are quite a few gift shops in town."

"Thanks, I'll try that." He left his number and walked back out into the sunshine. He hoped Daisy could find the lilacs. Frankie adored lilacs. He hadn't gotten any for her in forever. They'd had a lilac bush at their first tiny house in northern Georgia and she had loved it. She loved the scent of them. He'd been disappointed when they moved to Florida and he found out lilacs didn't grow in that climate.

Anyway, ordering the flowers was taken care of. That is if Daisy could find them. He hoped Frankie would be pleased. And he still needed that gift for her, too. Though she'd told him they weren't doing gifts for their anniversary because it would be inappropriate with how things were between them now. But he hadn't told Daisy that part. He still thought forty years should be celebrated. It was a long time. Maybe he could think of something small but meaningful. Like the lilacs.

He just hoped Frankie didn't get mad at him about the lilacs or the gift. But there was no telling with Frankie these days.

Frankie headed back to the cottage after spending time with the girls on the beach, grateful there was still no sign of Will. She'd just grab a quick shower, then maybe sit out on the porch and read for a bit. Stacey had stayed on the beach—probably getting a sunburn—and Katie went back to her cottage to work for a bit. Of course Katie was checking in with work on her vacation. That was just who she was.

Frankie took a shower, washing off the sand and sunscreen. She towel-dried her hair and then realized she hadn't brought her robe in with her. All she had was her damp swimsuit to put back on. That didn't appeal to her at all. Okay, this was silly. She could just wrap up in her towel and cross the hall to her room. Besides, hopefully Will wasn't even here.

She opened the door and tiptoed out right as Will walked out of his room. "Oh." His eyes widened.

"Uh, forgot my robe."

He just nodded but didn't take his eyes off her.

"I'll just... go to my room." She fled to her bedroom and closed the door behind her as her heart skipped a few beats. She leaned against the closed door. Now that was awkward. And she couldn't help but notice he didn't look away, but that was probably just because he was surprised. How enticing was an older woman with extra pounds wrapped up in a fluffy towel?

She dropped the towel to the floor and quickly got dressed, then went back to the bathroom to dry her hair and put on a bit of makeup. Will was nowhere to be seen. Maybe he'd gone over to the girls' cottage or down to the beach.

She grabbed her book and headed to the porch. She stopped abruptly when she saw Will sitting out there reading. "Ah, sorry. I didn't know you were out here."

"Just reading." He motioned to the other chair. "You could join me."

She wavered. Maybe she should just go back inside to her room and read.

"Frankie, really. It will be okay." He shook his head. "Surely we can sit on a porch together and read."

"Of course." She sank into the furthest chair from him, opened her book, and started reading. Not that she'd really call it reading because she stared at the page but soon realized she had no idea what the words said.

"You okay?" Will asked softly.

"What? Sure. I'm fine." She was so far from fine, it was ridiculous.

"I hope you can relax and just enjoy this week. It is nice to be having a vacation with the girls again, isn't it?"

"I am enjoying spending time with them."

"Frankie... I..." He shook his head. "Never mind. I'll let you get back to your book. I think I'll go take a walk on the beach."

She let out a long breath, glad he was leaving.

He noticed her look of relief, and a hurt expression flickered across his features before he hid it. A pang of guilt flashed through her. But really, she couldn't help herself. It was so hard to be around him, to endure the tension that swirled around them when they were together.

He set his book down on his chair and started toward the beach. He walked with long strides, his shoulders square, his hair blowing in the breeze. An incredibly handsome man. She used to feel his equal in the looks department, even though it was silly and shallow to compare. But now she was gray, overweight, and not in very good shape in spite of her best intentions to keep up with yoga or walks and watch her diet.

She looked across the courtyard at the colorful cottages. The memory of the faded cottages from their honeymoon flickered across her mind. Her heart clutched just thinking about the last time they were here. How had they gotten from that point to this one?

She just wanted things to be different now. Wanted to make something of her life other than being a wife and a mother. Oh, she'd worked a lot of jobs, but nothing that had been a career. Just jobs to bring in money. And it seemed like something always came up with the girls or with Will's work that made her eventually give up her job to be there for them. She always put them first.

But now, what did she have to show for her life? And what did Will think of her when he looked at her? He sure hadn't spent much time with her in the last five years or so. Even when he was home, he'd hurry off to the den to work.

She missed the way he used to look at her. Like he wanted her. How he'd reach out and capture her in his embrace and kiss her at random moments. She missed that. They used to do everything together. The crossword puzzle in the paper each evening after dinner. Special date nights. And he always looked at her as if he couldn't get enough of her. How she missed that look. And all the time they'd spend together. Sometimes they'd just sit for hours and talk about everything and nothing.

Pain seared through her for her loss. For their loss. Will had suggested talking to a therapist, but she didn't want to spill all her thoughts and feelings to some professional who would dissect them and tell her where she was wrong. Or insist they stay together. Isn't that what marriage counselors did? Explain why you needed to stay in the marriage?

She looked out toward the water.

Did she want to stay married?

That was the question, wasn't it? She just knew she couldn't live like this anymore. This charade of a marriage with the ghost of how it had been flitting around her.

CHAPTER 9

Frankie trailed behind Will and the girls down the pretty wharf stretching out over Moonbeam Bay. Customers wandered leisurely in and out of the shops and restaurants lining the wharf. Will turned and looked back at her. He slowed down, dropping behind the girls, waiting for her to catch up.

"Looks pretty different than when we came here on our honeymoon, doesn't it? It had just a few shops and maybe a couple restaurants back then."

"It looks very nice now. Love the twinkle lights strung across the wharf. They have all the benches lining the walkways now, too."

"Did you notice the marina when we walked

past? I swear it's three times the size it was back then."

"It has been a long time." Forty years. That was a long time.

Will stopped and reached out, gently catching her wrist. He looked directly into her eyes. "It has been a long time. We had lots of great years, didn't we?"

She swallowed and nodded.

"I know we've veered off track now, but maybe we could fix that."

She shook her head. "I... I don't think this is the time to talk about it. Look, the girls have stopped and are waiting for us. Come on, we should go." She pulled her wrist from his grasp.

They quickly caught up with the girls and continued to Jimmy's. They entered the restaurant and were shown to a table by the railing. She stood for a moment by the table, looking out at the harbor. The view here on the bay was breathtaking. The water stretched out before them. A few boats were moored out in the harbor, swaying gently with the motion of the tide.

"Oh, this is a good choice. Glad Violet suggested it," Katie said as she sat down next to

Stacey, leaving the two seats across from them for Will and her.

Will pulled out her chair and held it for her. She slipped into the seat and he sat down next to her. His shoulder brushed hers, but she ignored it and quietly scooted away from him so their shoulders no longer touched.

The waitress walked up with menus. "Hi, I'm Aspen. Welcome to Jimmy's. Have you been here before?"

"First time," Katie answered.

"Glad you decided to give us a try. May I take your drink orders and give you time to go over the menu?"

"How about a bottle of wine for the table? Red?" Will suggested.

"I'd prefer a white wine. A sauvignon blanc." She glanced down at the menu, but not before noticing the look on Will's face. But she wasn't just saying white because he suggested red. Well, probably not.

"I think I'll have a beer," Stacey said. "I see you have a local craft beer. I'll try that."

"It's great. Bet you'll like it."

"I'll try the beer, too," Katie ordered.

"Looks like just me for the red. Your house cab is fine."

"Okay, I'll bring those over to you right away."

Aspen walked over to the bar, and everyone tucked their heads, looking at the menu. "So many choices," Katie said.

There were a lot of choices, and everything looked wonderful. She knew Will would order the grouper. He loved that. Grouper blackened. She wasn't disappointed when Aspen returned and he ordered just that. They all placed their orders and sat sipping their drinks.

The conversation lagged. She took a deep breath, not wanting the girls to pick up on the awkwardness. "So, tomorrow is our shopping day?"

Katie's eyes lit up. "Yes, tomorrow. It will be fun. Dad, you don't mind if we have a girls' day, do you?"

"Not at all."

"Mom is going to take us shopping. You might feel your credit card melting." Stacey laughed.

"You all go and buy what you want. Hope you have a great time."

"We're going to help Mom pick out a new dress for the anniversary par—" Stacey choked. "The anniversary dinner."

"I don't need something new. I told you that." Repeatedly told them that, but no one was listening to her.

"Oh, come on. It will be fun to wear something new to the *dinner*." Katie eyed Stacey.

What was that all about? But anyway, she didn't really want to get a new dress but knew how Katie could be. She'd probably come back with a new dress in spite of her protests. Katie usually got her way. Oh, well, it was probably easier to get a new dress than to keep arguing.

"So what will you do all day, Dad?" Katie asked.

"I saw a bookshop in town. Think I'll drop by there and buy a new book. Almost finished the one I'm reading now."

"You and Mom and your reading. What do you think? A million books apiece per year?" Stacey shook her head. "I'm lucky if I read one or two. Much prefer movies."

"I prefer books." And so did Will. They'd spent hours together reading. In bed. On the couch. On the beach on vacation. One thing they had in common. Still had in common.

"We do both love to read," Will said. "And we like to take long walks. Or at least we used to."

They hadn't taken a long after-dinner walk in ages. Or read together, for that matter. Well, other than their awkward attempt this afternoon. She used to enjoy cuddling up to him, each with their own book. He'd lean over and kiss her sometimes, or just reach out to touch her, connect with her. But that hadn't happened in a very long time.

Aspen brought their meals and interrupted the conversation. As they ate, the girls mostly carried the discussion. Chatting about work. About what their friends from high school days were doing now. The new boutique opening in Sarasota they couldn't wait to see.

Will recounted endless stories of the girls when they were younger. Stacey learning to ride a bike… it took forever. Katie's first boyfriend, who Will gave a stern talking to before their first date. The year the Christmas tree fell on top of all the presents.

She smiled at the last story, surprised by how

relaxed she was with all the conversation. See, this wasn't so bad if she just let herself sit back and enjoy.

They ordered a big piece of chocolate cake to split even though she was stuffed. But a few bites wouldn't hurt anything, would it? So much for her diet.

As they finished their meal, Will stood and waited for her to get up. She rose, and they stood inches apart as they squeezed past the people sitting at the table behind them.

"Whoops, sorry," Will said as he bumped into her, and she ignored the quiver of sensation that flittered through her at his touch.

They followed the girls back out on the wharf. "So, does anyone want to grab a drink?" Stacey asked. "I saw a couple of places on our walk in."

"I do." Katie nodded.

Will turned to her. "Frankie?"

"Ah, I think I'm a bit tired. Fresh air and sunshine, I guess."

"That's fine. Katie and I can walk back to the cottages," Stacey said. "You take the car."

"Okay, then I'll drive your mother back now."

The girls stopped at an open-air bar and she and Will continued down the wharf. "That was a nice evening, wasn't it?" Will asked as they strolled along.

"It was." It had been surprisingly nice. Better than she'd anticipated. And for the first time in a long time, the tension wasn't stretching between them like a tall brick wall.

Will drove them back to the cottages, and they went inside. He dropped his keys on the counter and turned to her. "I picked up a bottle of red and a bottle of white when I was out running errands. Would you like to unwind with a drink? Here at the cottage where it's quiet instead of the noisy bar the girls went to?"

"I… uh…" Though, a glass of red did sound like a nice way to end the evening. So while her instinct was to say no to avoid spending time with him, her desire to unwind a bit more won. "Sure."

Will opened the wine and poured them each a glass. He handed her one and raised the other. "To a nice family dinner."

She clinked her glass against his and took a sip, remembering all the toasts he'd made through the years. To their first child, their second, the girls' first steps, his first promotion, and their move to Florida. And so many more.

She turned and walked over to the sofa, sinking down on its beckoning cushions. Will took a seat next to her, but not too close. Not like before, when he'd sit right beside her and wrap his arm around her.

"You doing okay with all this? This week, I mean." His eyebrow rose. "I know you were worried."

"I'm doing okay. And... and I'm glad we decided to come. It will make a great memory."

"We have lots of memories, Francine. Lots of them."

He leaned over and brushed a lock of her hair away from her face. She could feel the heat of his hand when he did it. But he quickly pulled his hand back. "Sorry, instinctive move." He gave her the tiniest smile.

She took a sip of her wine, a bit shaken at the small gesture.

"You look great tonight, by the way. Wanted to tell you earlier before we left, but you looked... nervous."

A small laugh escaped her lips. "I was nervous, which is silly. Just dinner with the girls."

His lips curved up in a smile. "Haven't heard your laugh in a long time. I've missed it."

She didn't laugh much now. Or smile. In her confusion about life, about what she needed, about everything, she just... existed now. She frowned.

"Now you're frowning."

"I... ah. You're right. I haven't laughed much. My mind is just so full of... thinking." That sounded lame.

He set his wine down and took her hand in his. "I know you're trying to figure things out. How you feel. I'm sorry I haven't been there for you like you needed. Sorry I didn't put our marriage first. It got lost in the girls and my work and... I'm just so sorry."

"I know... but it doesn't change anything, does it? Sorry doesn't."

"No, an apology doesn't change things. But I still wanted you to know. Say it out loud to you."

"I'm sorry things are the way they are now, too. I just need... space." She pulled her hand from his, took a last sip of her wine, and rose. "I better head to bed. I'm beat."

She hurried down the hall, got ready for

bed, and climbed in, piling the pillows behind her as she sat there. Hot tears began to flow as she silently cried, mourning the past. Mourning how it had been.

Will sat on the sofa, sipping his wine after Frankie went to bed. Sadness curled around him, smothering him. He'd had just a brief moment tonight of talking and feeling close to Frankie again. A brief hope that maybe, maybe, they could work things out. But nothing he said seemed to change anything. She always pulled away.

And at this point, if she needed space, he knew he should give it to her. But it tore at his heart to think of moving out of the home they'd lived in for so many years. He was afraid of what would happen if he did.

Afraid it was a step in the wrong direction. That he'd never be moving back in again.

Frankie looked so beautiful tonight. Her dress had picked up the amber flecks in her eyes. The breeze off the harbor had made locks of her hair dance around, framing her face. And the haunted look in her eyes had started to wane as they all enjoyed their dinner at Jimmy's.

He should tell her how beautiful she is more often. He knew she thought she was overweight and kept saying how she was going to dye her gray hair, but he still thought she was so attractive. The wrinkles only showed she'd lived a good life, and the smile lines were deeper now —when she actually smiled.

He stood up and took the two glasses to the sink and washed them, setting them on the dish rack to dry. He turned and looked around the room, taking in the comfortable sofa, the airy beach painting on the wall, and the well-worn but sparkling clean floors. A room decorated to be a cozy place to hang out.

But it didn't feel cozy without Frankie.

But the one thing she'd asked of him, he could do that for her. He could give her the space she wanted. He would give her that. Give her anything she needed. She deserved that. She deserved the world.

And certainly a man better than he was. Someone who treated her like she was the most important thing in his life.

And the sad thing was... Frankie *was* the

most important person in his life. He just hadn't taken the time to show that to her.

An idea formed, and he filled with determination, certain now of what he could do for her. How he could prove he was listening to her and what she said she needed.

CHAPTER 10

Frankie slipped out for an early beach walk the next morning. She'd heard Will stirring in his room and wanted to get out before he came out. Even though she was starting to feel a bit more relaxed around him on this trip, it was still hard. She walked a long way down the beach, lost in thought, before turning around and heading back.

Rose was sitting in the same spot as yesterday and waved as she approached. "Good morning, Frankie."

"Morning, Rose."

"Want to join me for a bit?"

It did sound better than heading inside the

cottage, so she dropped down on the sand beside Rose.

"Just taking a little time to enjoy the morning? I find a nice beach walk is a good time to think."

Think. That's exactly what she'd done with each and every step. About Will. The girls. Their life. How she felt like the universe was trying to squeeze her and suck all her breath away.

"You okay?" Rose's forehead creased.

She laughed ruefully and shook her head. "Yes, I'm okay. I was just thinking about what I'd been thinking about." That sounded convoluted, but she was overthinking every little detail of her life.

Rose smiled. "Want to talk about it?"

"I... ah..." Rose was a total stranger. How could she explain all this to her?

"Sometimes it helps to talk."

"It's just... it's Will and my fortieth anniversary. And..." She paused and scooped up a handful of sand, letting it sift through her fingers. "You see, we've talked about separating. Well, I've talked about it. Will doesn't really want to. And our girls know nothing about this.

They've planned this anniversary trip, and we didn't want to spoil it for them."

"I see." Rose nodded.

"And now everything is just so confusing. I feel like there is no me anymore. That Will doesn't see me. He hasn't seen me in forever."

"Have you told him that?"

"Well, not in so many words. I tried to talk to him a few times, but we got into big arguments. And we never argue." She shrugged. "I get so mad at him, and I just… walk away from the argument. We never solve anything. There is so much tension between us. It's like I can't relax around him. Can't enjoy anything. It's hard to even relax and enjoy this vacation with the girls. Although I did have a good time on the beach with just the girls yesterday, and dinner last night was nice after I finally relaxed."

"Maybe you can just enjoy the little moments on the trip. Time with the girls. Family time. Some of the moments have to be bringing you joy. And you know, it's really the little moments that matter in life. Those ordinary, extraordinary moments."

And when had she forgotten how to enjoy

the little moments? She was so wrapped up in her problems, her feelings, her thoughts. But then, her whole relationship with Will dangled over her head all the time.

"So, why do you want to separate from Will, if you don't mind me asking?"

"I can't breathe when I'm around him anymore. So much tension. He's ignored me for so many years. He... he doesn't look at me like he used to. Like he... like he wants me. I mean, I don't blame him for that. I've put on all this weight." She patted her stomach. "My hair is gray. I've got wrinkles. And he just keeps getting more handsome as he ages."

"Maybe he thinks you look more beautiful as you age."

She shook her head. "I don't think so."

"You should talk to him. Really talk to him. A heart to heart."

"I've tried, but we just end up getting defensive and... well, I usually walk away from it."

"A counselor might help."

"I don't want to be told I should try this or that to keep our marriage..." She looked out at the water. "Because… I don't know if I *want* to keep our marriage."

"Forty years is a long time. And people do change. My Emmett and I changed a lot over the years. But we swore we'd always talk things out. Even if one of us wanted something different as we aged. Do you want something different… different for you? Aside from you and Will?"

"I do. I look back at my life and I was Will's wife and the girls' mother. Is that all I have to show for my life?"

"Raising two girls to adulthood is something to be proud of. I'm sure Will owes some of his success in business to all you did to help him."

"I just feel like… there should be more, you know?"

"How about finding a job or even some worthy volunteer activity?"

"My jobs have all been just that. Jobs, not careers. And without much experience, who is going to hire me?"

"Any job you particularly liked?"

"I did work in admin for the children's foundation for a while. I enjoyed that. It's such a worthy cause. And we'd have an annual

Christmas party for the kids. They all got a stack of presents. Some of them for the first time."

"So why don't you see if they need a volunteer? Or if they have a job opening?"

She looked over at Rose. How had a complete stranger come up with the most appealing idea in all this time she'd been trying to figure things out?

"You know, that is a good idea. I'd enjoy that." She was going to grab her phone and look up the foundation when she got back to the cottage. See who was running it now and talk to them. And if not that foundation, maybe another one. Maybe if she found a position doing work that had meaning, she'd feel... fulfilled.

"You know, you don't really need outside validation, though." Rose interrupted her thoughts. "You just have to believe you are worthy. That you matter. That is what's important. Believe in yourself."

She sat there for a bit, letting Rose's words sink in. Was she trying to get validation from Will? Or from some job? Did she need that?

"You know, my Emmett and I never had children. And there was a time when I was certain I should leave him and give him a chance to find a woman who could give him children. But Emmett wouldn't hear of it. He wanted me more than he wanted children. We talked it through. I bet you and Will could sit down and if you opened up about your true feelings, maybe you could work things out. It might not be easy, and change is hard, but it might be worth it for you. And promise yourself you won't walk away in the middle of the conversation if it gets tough."

She bit her lip and stared out at the waves, slowly rolling to the shore. Rose was a wise, wise woman. Frankie stood and brushed the sand from her shorts. "You've given me a lot to think about, Rose. Thank you for talking with me."

"You're welcome. I'm here every morning. Just drop on by. The door is always open." Rose's eyes twinkled.

Frankie turned and headed back to the cottage. So much to think about. It wasn't time to talk to Will now. Not while they were on this vacation. Besides, she needed some time to process all that Rose had said. But she was determined to tell him they should talk when they got back home. Or pretty determined. It was the right thing to do, wasn't it? Was Rose right?

The girls were sitting on the porch of their cottage as she walked up. "Mom! Come join us."

She climbed the stairs to their porch and Katie went in to grab her a cup of coffee. She sank onto a chair beside them as the girls chattered about their upcoming shopping trip. She relaxed in her chair while the girls talked, chiming in when they asked her questions, just enjoying spending this time with them.

She glanced over at the spot on the beach where she and Rose had talked. Rose was right about this, too. Enjoy the little moments in life. The extraordinary, ordinary moments. Just like this one.

CHAPTER 11

Melody went in for the morning shift at Sea Glass Cafe, trying to keep busy. Trying to keep from worrying about her date tonight with Ethan. It wasn't really working.

Ethan walked in and took a table like he did most days. She grabbed a menu—not that he needed it—and headed over to his table.

"Morning." She dropped the menu. "Oops, sorry." She bent to pick it up and hand it to him.

"Hey." Ethan looked up at her with a wide smile on his lips. "Came in for breakfast and…" He paused and tilted his head, throwing her a small smile. "Making sure we're still on for tonight."

She briefly considered telling him she had to

work, but that was an outright lie. Evelyn had done a happy dance when she told her that she was going out with Ethan. No way Evelyn would let her work tonight.

"Of course, we're still on." She pasted on a smile. "Looking forward to it." *Liar, liar, pants on fire.*

"I'd understand if you wanted to—"

"Back out? Bail on you? Chicken out?" She laughed. A nervous laugh, but a laugh nonetheless. "No, we're all set." Did that sound confident?

"Great. I'll pick you up at six. Cabot Hotel restaurant still sound okay?"

"Sounds great." She wrote down his order and took the menu from him, holding it firmly in her grasp as she hurried back to the kitchen.

Evelyn looked up from where she was placing a pie on the counter. "You okay? You looked a bit flushed."

"I'm fine. I just waited on Ethan. He thought I might back out of our date tonight."

Evelyn raised her eyebrows. "And did you?"

"Of course not." She shook her head from side to side but didn't admit she'd thought about it.

"Good. Because it's about time you went out with him. He's had a thing for you forever."

"Why does everyone keep saying that?"

Evelyn laughed. "Because it's the truth."

Melody headed back out and waited on another table of customers, spilling water as she poured their glasses. She quickly mopped up her mess and apologized. What was wrong with her today?

She headed back to the kitchen, yet again, and grabbed Ethan's meal. "Enjoy," She said as she set it down on the table and eyed his water glass wondering if she should chance filling it.

"Can you join me?"

She looked around the room. "Kind of busy."

"Okay, sure, that's okay." He looked kind of disappointed though.

They weren't really ridiculously busy, and she could probably sit down for a few minutes, but she was so jittery. Then the door opened and some new customers came in, justifying her decision.

Ethan ate his breakfast and left, and luckily the lunch rush soon kept her busy. Evelyn finally chased her out of the cafe early in the afternoon. "Scoot. Go home and get ready for your date."

"I could fill those salt shakers before I leave."

"Nope."

"Do up that stack of dirty dishes?"

"I've got those."

She sighed and hung up her apron. "I shouldn't really be this nervous, should I?"

"No, you shouldn't. But you can't help the way you feel. I hope you can just relax and have a great time. And I can't wait to hear all about it tomorrow."

"Okay, I'll go." She wanted to grab a shower and then attempt to do something with her hair. But what? She usually just pulled it back at the restaurant. Maybe she'd do something a bit fancier for tonight? If she could even remember how to do it. And she did have the dress Violet helped her pick out.

"Have fun," Evelyn called out encouragingly.

She headed out the door and down the sidewalk, looking down at her watch to check the time. Without work to keep her busy, the minutes were just going to slowly tick away, mocking her.

Enough of that crazy thinking. She'd have fun with Ethan. She was *fine*. Everything would be fine.

CHAPTER 12

Frankie checked out the children's foundation and found out a friend of hers, Mary, was now running it. She couldn't remember the last time she'd seen Mary. But then, she hadn't seen many of her friends the last year. She sent off an email to her, asking about any possible openings at the foundation, typing carefully on her phone. She much preferred typing on a laptop but hadn't brought hers with her on vacation.

Will left to go run errands. He sure running errands a lot on vacation, but maybe he was just keeping busy and giving her space. Still, it felt a bit like he was avoiding her. Which was crazy talk because she'd *asked* him to give her space.

She shook her head. She really was a silly goose these days. Silly goose. Her mother used to say that phrase. Why had it popped up now? She hurried back to her room and got ready for a day of shopping, sure she'd be coming back with a new dress if Katie had her way.

She and the girls headed to Portside Grill for lunch. It almost seemed like old times. Lunch with the girls. Laughing. Talking. She should ask them to go to lunch with her more often after they all got home. This last year she'd been so wrapped up in her problems that she hadn't gotten together with the girls as much as she should have. Or her friends. That was going to change.

After lunch, they wandered down Magnolia Avenue and headed into Barbara's Boutique and were greeted by the owner.

"You must be Barbara," Stacey said.

The woman laughed. "No, I'm Margaret. The shop hasn't been owned by Barbara in years, but the name stuck."

"We're here looking for a dress for Mom," Katie said.

Margaret led them over to racks full of dresses. "Let me know if I can help you."

"Oh, Mom, look at this dress. It would be perfect." Katie held up a dress and picked up another one. "Or this one."

"Katie, I thought I was taking you two shopping." She looked over to where Stacey was browsing dresses in her own size.

"Oh, come on. Let's find something for you."

Frankie tried on the dresses that Katie insisted she look at. She finally gave in and selected a pretty lilac-colored dress. Her favorite color. It was simple, and as a bonus, it hid her stomach, so she was pleased with that.

"See, Mom. I told you we'd find you the perfect dress."

"How about we find one for you?"

"I… uh. I found one back home. Two actually." Katie laughed. "Couldn't make up my mind. Guess I'll have to decide before Saturday."

"You said we have reservations at the restaurant in The Cabot Hotel?"

"Uh… yes. I said that." Katie turned away and pick up a purse. "This is cute, isn't it?"

"It is. I'll buy it for you."

"No, I meant for you."

"The dress is fine. That's all I need." And she didn't really *need* the dress.

She paid for her dress, the purse for Katie, and two dresses Stacey picked out for herself. They headed outside, carrying their packages.

"That was a fun afternoon, wasn't it?" She felt light and relaxed and reveled in the feeling.

"It was great," Stacey said as she slid into the car. "Thanks for the dresses."

"You really didn't need to buy me this purse," Katie added.

"And I didn't really need this dress." She smiled at her daughter. "But here we both are with our packages."

They headed back to the cottages, and she saw their car parked out front. Will must be back from his running around. That was good. Because she was going to tell him they should sit down and talk after this week was over. Rose was right. They did need to discuss everything. How she felt. What they could do to... to fix things. Was that what she wanted? To fix things?

She slipped out of the car. "I'll see you girls

in a bit. We'll have to decide where to go to dinner."

"I've got a list of places to go," Katie said.

Of course she did. She grinned as she climbed the stairs, eager to talk to Will. At least tell him they should talk. She wasn't quite ready to have the discussion while they were here on this trip, but just knowing they'd talk after they got home lightened her mood. Her heart skipped as she opened the door. For the first time in a long time, she thought she was at least making progress. That maybe things might turn around. That maybe she was headed on the right path. If they could talk without arguing. If things could change.

She went inside and found Will standing by the sink, a glass of water in his hand.

"Looks like you had a successful shopping trip." He nodded toward her package.

"You know how it's no use arguing with Katie when she gets her mind set on something. The dress is pretty, though." She set the bag down on a chair. "Did you get your running around all done?"

"I... I did. And I wanted to talk to you."

"I want to talk to you, too." She walked over and rested a hip on the counter. "You first."

"I've been thinking about all you've said. How tense everything has been between us. And the only thing you asked is for me to move out."

"I—"

He held up a hand and cut her off. "No, I get it. You need time to think. Without all the tension that's been building and building between us. Frankie, I'd give you anything you needed. Anything." He set his glass down. "So I drove back up to Sarasota and signed a lease on a condo. I'm moving next week. Everything is all set. You'll get what you need."

She stared at his face for a moment. The face that she knew every line, every curve. The dimples that deepened when he smiled. But not now. A sad expression hovered in his eyes, but he looked... proud of himself? Was that it? Maybe.

She turned and walked over to the table and sank into a chair. He'd finally done what she'd asked of him. He was moving out to give her space. Then why had the announcement sucked the air from her lungs? Why had heartache hammered down on her?

Will walked over and sat in the chair beside her. "It's a furnished place so I won't need to take any furniture or anything. You'll still have it all. I hope this helps, Frankie. I truly do."

Now was the time to tell him she wanted to talk to him after they got back home. But then, he'd already made plans to move out. Maybe that was a good thing. Time apart might help them both. Isn't that what she wanted? Maybe she should take some time for herself and they could talk after she'd had that time alone.

Will looked at her closely. "Anyway, I hope knowing I'm moving out will ease some of the tension this week. Let you just enjoy the vacation. And you can see I'm actually listening to you. Giving you what you need."

She nodded slowly. "Yes… thank you." She rose and picked up her package. "I think I'm going to go lie down for a bit before dinner." She headed back to her bedroom.

Things just got more and more confusing. Will had finally done what she asked. She should be happy, shouldn't she?

Rose's words came back to her. *Talk to him. Really talk. And don't let yourself walk away from the conversation.*

CHAPTER 13

K atie looked at the clock. "You about ready, Stacey?" Her sister was known for being late. Which is why she'd told her sister to be ready fifteen minutes before the time she'd texted her mother to be ready.

Stacey came out of her room and grabbed her purse. "I'm ready."

Fourteen minutes late, but that meant they'd be over to their parents' cottage right on time. "Come on." She led the way next door, climbed the stairs, and knocked twice before opening the door. "We're here."

Her mother came walking into the front room looking lovely, but a bit tired. Guess all that shopping had worn her out. Her eyes looked… sad? But she was certain her mother had a good time. Fairly certain. She glanced over at Stacey, but her sister was busy texting on her phone. Great, text people instead of enjoying your family time. Annoyed, she turned back to her mom. "I picked this great-sounding place to go. Not too far. Just over on Belle Island. It's called Magic Cafe. Supposed to be wonderful. Right on the beach."

"Sounds wonderful, honey." Her mother's eyes didn't quite light up with the anticipation Katie expected.

"Hey, can I use the bathroom? Stacey was hogging ours. Just need to touch up my hair for a sec."

"Was not." Stacey looked up from her phone, glared at her, and went back to texting.

"Sure, go ahead, honey."

Katie headed down the hallway. She glanced at the bedroom on the left. Her mother had spread an outfit out on the bed but was still wearing what she'd had on when they went shopping. She took another step and ran into her father coming out of the room on the right.

She glanced behind him and saw his things on the dresser, a shirt hanging on the back of a chair. She frowned.

"What's this? Separate rooms?" She looked up at her dad, then glanced back toward her mom.

Her dad cleared his throat. "I... I was just giving your mother some more room. It's a queen bed. We're used to a king."

"So... on your anniversary trip, you're sleeping separately?" She didn't understand. Her parents had never been the sleep-in-separate-rooms type of people.

"Hey, Katie, not really your place to ask that." Stacey finally slipped her phone into her pocket.

Katie walked back toward her mom. "Is something wrong? You both have been acting strange. Different." Her heart sped up as she saw a look of panic cross her mother's face. "Mom?"

Her dad crossed the distance and stood beside her mom, looking down at her. Waiting. What was he waiting for?

"Frankie?" He eyed her mom.

Her heart pounded as she stood there staring at them, waiting for one of them to talk. To explain.

~

Will stood there looking intently at her with questioning eyes. Frankie sighed.

She didn't want this moment to continue. She just wanted to lie to the girls and tell them everything was fine. But lying right to their face when they would find out soon enough? It was one thing not to tell them when they hadn't been asking questions. But now?

"Frankie, they'll find out next week, anyway." Will nudged her gently.

She looked up at him and nodded, her heart hammering, and she steadied herself for their reaction. But she couldn't find the words.

Will stared at her for a moment and turned toward Katie and Stacey. "Girls…" He paused for a moment as if gathering strength. "Your mother and I… Well…"

"Dad, what is it?" Katie's forehead creased with a frown, her expression wary.

"Your mother and I have decided to... separate."

"What?" Stacey's eyes widened. "You're joking. You two are like the picture-perfect married couple."

"Really? Separate? You're going to separate? Like live in two different places?" Katie's eyes clouded.

"Yes, we just need... some space," Will said without blaming it all on her, which she was forever grateful for.

"But you can't separate. We have a whole party planned for your anniversary," Stacey wailed.

"What?" she said in perfect unison with Will.

Katie glared at Stacey. "Way to go."

She turned to Katie. "What is Stacey talking about?"

Katie let out a long sigh. "We kind of planned a surprise anniversary party for you. Your friends are coming down. We planned to have it here in the courtyard."

"You did all that for your mother and me?" A bewildered expression settled on Will's face as he tried to take it all in.

"I'm sorry. I had no idea about… this. About you two." Katie held up her hands. "I guess we can contact everyone and cancel."

Frankie looked at Will. "What do you think? I don't really want to cancel and have everyone know we're having… problems."

"I think forty years is still something to celebrate. Celebrate that we made this wonderful family with you two amazing girls."

Stacey looked at her, then Will, then shook her head. "I can't believe you're doing this. I can't." She whirled around and raced from the cottage, slamming the door behind her.

"I'm sorry you two had to find out like this. We were going to tell you after this week." She reached out and took Katie's hand.

"I'm sorry, too, Mom." Katie was fighting back tears, her words coming out in choked syllables. "I'm sorry you both feel you need to separate. But I really hope you can work things out." A sob escaped Katie as she dashed her hand to swipe at a tear she couldn't hold back. "Maybe we should, uh, cancel dinner tonight."

"That's probably a good idea." Will reached out and placed his hand on Katie's shoulder to comfort her.

"I think I'll go find Stacey. See if she's okay."
Katie touched Will's hand, then turned and
scurried out the door.

Frankie sank onto the wooden chair by the
table. "Well, that was unexpected."

"I hate seeing them hurt. It has to be such a
shock to them."

"I'm sure it was. And our timing… it's really
lousy, isn't it?" She stared down at her hands
resting in her lap. Her wedding ring caught her
eye, mocking her.

Will shook his head, his eyes sad and tinged
with pain. "When is a good time to tell your kids
you're separating, Frankie?"

"I—" But what could she answer to that?

"I'm going to go take a walk." Will turned
and disappeared out the door and she sat there
all alone. Terribly, terribly alone.

Katie fought back her tears. She hated to cry.
Always had. She stood outside taking in long,
controlling breaths as she slowly got her tears
under control.

She squared her shoulders and headed back

to her cottage. She found Stacey sitting on the couch, tears running down her face. She crossed over and plopped down on the couch beside her. "You okay?"

"No, I'm not okay. Of course not. Our parents are getting divorced."

"You don't know that. Maybe they just need some time to work things out."

Stacey glared at her. "How many people do you know who separate and then get back together? And what in the world has come over them? They don't fight. They've been married for forty years. Forty. Doesn't that mean anything anymore?"

"I think all couples have problems now and then."

"I'm so mad at them. Why didn't they try harder? And why now? Right when we planned this big party for them. We've done all this work."

"I don't think they planned it this way." Leave it to Stacey to make it all about her, not that she'd actually *done* that much for the party.

"So we're going to have to pretend that everything is just hunky-dory at the party. Pretend our parents aren't going back home to different places? And then what happens when everyone finds out? You know they will. They'll think we were ridiculous for having the anniversary party. Or think we were clueless for not knowing what was coming."

"Stacey, this isn't about you. Or me. And I'm sure Mom and Dad are having a hard time with all of this, too." She said the words more sharply than she meant to. But sometimes Stacey could be so self-centered. And she'd seen her parents' eyes. They were filled with pain. She wasn't sure what was causing all this, but she was certain it was hard on them.

Stacey jumped up off the couch. "You know, this affects us, too. A lot. Like the holidays. How are those going to work out? And do you realize this is our last family vacation? Everything is changing. Everything." Stacey wheeled around and slammed out of the cottage.

Katie sank back on the couch and silence surrounded her. A lonely silence. A sad silence. Stacey was right that things would change for them. But it was changing for their parents too. She couldn't imagine what had happened to cause them to want to separate.

They always seemed so happy. Well, Dad

had been super busy the last few years. Out of town a lot. And she knew her mother had a hard time with the whole empty nest thing.

Maybe they had just grown apart. People do.

But couldn't they try to find their way back to each other? To the people they'd grown into? Had they tried? Gone to a counselor?

Had one of them cheated?

Dad had been out of town a lot. Wasn't that classic for a cheating husband? Or had Mom gotten lonely being there at home all alone and found someone else?

She felt guilty even thinking it. She couldn't imagine either of them cheating, though.

But then, she'd never in a million years have thought her parents would separate. So what did she know?

She got up and paced the room. Cleaned up some dirty dishes Stacey had left out on the counter. Paced some more.

What had happened with her parents? What was so impossible to fix that Dad had to move out?

Sadness swept through her. For the pain her

parents obviously were going through. For the feeling that their family was breaking into tiny little pieces. She was a fixer, a helper... but there wasn't really anything she could do to fix this.

CHAPTER 14

Melody looked at the three new dresses she'd gotten when she went shopping with Violet. The teal one was Violet's favorite and hers too. She reached into the closet and took it out, spreading it out on her bed.

She looked at her watch, glared at it, certain it must be broken. How had this afternoon stretched out so long in slow, measured minutes? Her hair hung in damp clumps around her shoulders. She still needed to dry it and style it. For once she wished she were one of those women who could fix their hair up in a style with loose tendrils drifting down and it would look like she did it on purpose, not like her hair was all falling out of a misshapen bun.

She went into the bathroom and swiped away the last of the steam on the mirror. Grabbing the hair dryer, she plugged it in and started the process. Using a bit of product on her hair—when was the last time she'd done that?—she started drying it, using a round brush to curl it. When she was finished, she thought she'd done a pretty good job. She debated hitting the curls with some hair spray, but she hated the way it made her hair feel. This would just have to do and hopefully the curls would hold for the evening.

She went back into the bedroom and slipped on the dress. It really was pretty. It made her *feel* pretty. Something she hadn't felt in a long time. Not because of any reason except she hadn't really thought about it. Hadn't thought about how she looked. She just got up, went to work, and came home. She was proud of how much she'd learned while working at the cafe. And she loved working there. Loved making enough money to support herself since John died.

And there he was. Standing right there in the room with her. She swore she could almost reach out and touch him. She was crazy, but she couldn't help herself...

"Hey, babe. You okay with this? With me going on a date?" She spoke into the empty room.

Of course, the mirage didn't answer her. She shook her head at her craziness and walked over to the dresser. She sorted through her jewelry and picked out a necklace to wear. In the back of the drawer, half-hidden under a scarf, a piece of paper was poking out.

She scooted the scarf over and picked up the slip of paper as her heart started to hammer in her chest.

A note from John. He'd always left her little notes scattered around the house. In the kitchen cabinet. In the container of coffee. In the pocket of a jacket. Her breath caught as she slowly read the words.

Hey gorgeous, have a great day.

She clutched the paper to her chest. Was John giving her his blessing to go out? She read it again, certain now that John would be okay with this. He'd want her to be happy, just like she'd want John to find someone new if their situation was reversed.

She smoothed the note and set it on the dresser. She'd have to add it to the shoebox stuffed full of all the notes he'd written her. But for now, she'd leave it out and read it often.

The doorbell rang, and she took a sharp intake of breath. She kissed her fingers and lightly pressed them to the note. "Thank you, John." With one last look in the mirror, she headed to open the door.

Ethan stood in the doorway with a bouquet of flowers in his hands. "Here, these are for you."

She took the bouquet. "They're beautiful."

"I know you love flowers. I just thought… it might be a good way to start the evening." Ethan shifted from foot to foot.

"Oh, come in. Come in. Sorry. Let me put them in a vase." She hurried to the kitchen, found her favorite vase, filled it with water, and set the flowers in it. She brought it back out and set it on a table in the front room, adjusting the delicate flowers until they looked just right. Then fiddled with them again.

"They look nice." Ethan still stood just a few feet inside the doorway.

"They do. Thank you."

"Oh, and I meant to say when I first saw you. You look great."

"Thanks."

Ethan gave a little laugh. "I'm sorry. I'm so nervous. Haven't been on a date in a long, long time."

"Me either."

"Guess we'll just have to relearn how to do it together." His lips curved into a smile.

For some reason, it calmed her nerves to know he was just as uneasy about tonight as she was.

Ethan drove them to The Cabot Hotel, and they walked into the elegant lobby. Delbert Hamilton, the owner who had recently purchased the hotel and renovated it, saw them and waved. They walked over to where he was standing by the reception desk.

"Mr. Hamilton, hello," she greeted him.

He smiled at her. "Hello, Melody. And how many times must I insist you call me Delbert?"

"I'll try to remember."

"And, Ethan, good evening."

"Good evening, sir."

Delbert shook his head. "And it's Delbert to you, too. Sir is… well, I'd rather be your friend." He smiled. "You two here for dinner?"

"We are." She nodded.

"Come on. Let me make sure you get one of our best tables." Delbert led them to the restaurant, and they were promptly seated at a table by the large windows overlooking the harbor.

The waitress brought them menus and said she'd be back for their drink order.

"What would you like to drink?" Ethan asked.

"I don't drink very often. I'm not sure."

"Tonight seems like a celebration of sorts, doesn't it? They have a split of champagne. We could get that. Does that sound good?"

"Yes, that sounds lovely." And he was right. Tonight did feel like a celebration. A step toward getting back into life again after losing John.

They got their champagne and ordered their meals. Ethan raised his glass. "To our first date and our friendship."

That was the perfect toast as far as she was concerned. She raised her glass and lightly touched it to Ethan's. He'd said first date. Did that mean he planned on more dates? And suddenly that didn't seem like such a bad idea.

Their meals came and her seafood risotto

smelled delicious. Ethan's snapper looked great, too. The meals were professionally plated with a bit of garnish on each plate. Rather different from the cafe. Though the Sea Glass Cafe's food was excellent, she quickly defended the restaurant that she owed her loyalty to.

"Bet it's nice to sit and let someone else cook and wait on you for a change." Ethan glanced over at her. "You're always cooking or waiting on people at the cafe."

"It is nice. I mean, I love my job, but this is really nice."

They chatted easily as they ate their meals. She was surprised at how relaxed she was and how smoothly the evening was going. All that worry for nothing. She should have remembered how easy Ethan was to be around, to talk to.

They finished their meal and their last sips of champagne. Ethan rose. "Want to go out to the pavilion? Looks like the moon is putting on a show over the harbor."

"Yes, let's. It's beautiful out tonight."

He took her hand in his, then quickly looked at her. "That's okay?" He nodded down at their hands.

"Yes, it's fine." Emotions swelled through

her at having a man hold her hand again. But her hand felt comfortable in Ethan's, felt right, as they walked along in the moonlight.

They went to the edge of the pavilion and looked out over the water. The moon splashed a trail of silvery light across the bay. Stars twinkled above them. A light breeze blew her hair around her shoulders—probably loosening all her curls—but she didn't mind.

He reached over and gently swept a lock of her hair back from her face. She swallowed hard at the look of smokey desire in his eyes. But his lips just lifted into a gentle smile and he took his hand back.

She glanced at her watch, surprised to see they'd been on their date for over three hours. "I guess we should head back. I have the early shift tomorrow."

"Of course." He took her hand back in his and led her to his car.

When they got back to her house, he jumped out and came around to open her car door. She slipped out and stood oh so close to him. Her breath caught in her throat, but he stepped back to let her pass.

He took her hand, and they slowly walked up the steps to her house. She looked down at her hand entwined with his, then up into his eyes. His eyes brimmed with tenderness edged with passion. She swallowed and stepped back slightly.

"That was fun tonight. Better than I thought." The heat of a blush crept across her face. "No, I didn't mean it that way. I just meant…"

He laughed. "That you were nervous?"

"Yes, that. It was strange to date someone after so long."

"But you did have a good time, right?" His eyes widened, questioning her, and he tilted his head.

"I really did."

Relief hovered over his features. "So now that the whole first date thing is behind us, we could go out again."

She looked at him, his eyes shining with expectation. "Yes, I think we could. I'd like that."

His lips broke into a wide grin. "Great. How soon?"

She laughed. "I'm off on Sunday. We could

go on a picnic in the afternoon if you'd like. I make a great picnic basket."

He nodded eagerly. "I'd love that."

"I guess I should go in."

"Yes, I should go." Ethan walked down the steps and turned back to her. "Melody?"

"Yes?"

"Can I tell you something?"

"Of course. You can tell me anything."

"I… I was going to kiss you, but chickened out." He chuckled and hurried off to his car.

She tried to suppress a laugh but didn't quite succeed and waved at him as he pulled away. She wasn't sure if she was glad he'd chickened out or not.

CHAPTER 15

K atie walked out onto the porch of her cottage, sipping on a cup of coffee. The morning sunshine spilled across the courtyard, promising a gorgeous day. The morning didn't seem to realize her family's lives had been blown apart yesterday.

She glanced over at her parents' cottage just as her father walked outside. He spied her and lifted a hand in a wave. She trotted over and climbed the stairs. "Morning, Dad."

"Want a refill on your coffee? I can make some more."

"No, thanks. I already had a couple of cups. Been up for a while. Couldn't sleep."

Her dad smiled ruefully. "Must be going around. I couldn't either."

"Is Mom still sleeping?" She cut off her words. Why would she ask him that? It wasn't like he was sleeping in the same room as her mother.

"I... I don't think so. I think she's gone. Probably out on a walk. She seems to be enjoying early morning walks since we got here."

Katie sucked in a deep breath. "So, Dad... can we talk?"

"Of course. Anytime. You know that."

"I wanted to talk about you and Mom. What happened? Why are you moving out? I just don't understand."

He sank into a chair and set his coffee down on the table beside him. "Well... it's what your mother wants. What she asked me to do. And I'd do anything she wants at this stage. We've grown apart. Almost like we live separate lives. I've been a lousy husband to her the last several years. Okay, a lot of years. Haven't given her what she needed. Ignored her and used the excuse that I was so busy with work. No woman deserves to be treated like that."

"But can't you change now?"

"I'm trying, sweetie. I am. But for right now, I'm giving your mother what she asked for. I'm really listening to her... something she's always accused me of not doing. I'm listening to what she needs."

"But to move out? It sounds so... final."

"I hope it's not. I hope, given time, your mother will give me another chance. If I can show her that things will be different. If we can work things out."

"Oh, Dad. I'm just so sad for you. For Mom. For all of us."

"I am, too. But I have to do what's best for your mother. And she thinks this is best."

"Do you think..." She couldn't believe she was even asking this question. "Uh, have you talked about divorce?"

He stared down into his coffee cup before replying, "No, that word hasn't been said. But I worry Frankie has thought about it. And I don't know what I'd do without her in my life. She's my... everything."

"Then you should prove it to her, Dad."

"I should. And I should have been showing her all along how important she was to me.

How important she still is to me. How much I care. That I think she's still the most beautiful woman I know." He let out a long sigh. "I've made so many mistakes. So many."

"But we learn from our mistakes, don't we?"

"We do. I sure have. I'm just not sure if I can fix this one. We've drifted so far apart. I might have let it go on too long."

"I hope not. I hope you two can work it out."

He gave her a wry smile. "Me, too. And I'm sorry about the timing of all this. I know you went to a lot of trouble to arrange this vacation and the anniversary party. And your mother and I do appreciate it."

She stared into her now empty coffee cup. "Yes, the timing is unfortunate. But honestly, it wasn't ever going to be a good time to hear about this. We'll make the best of it at the party. It might be awkward, but we'll work it out. I promise."

He pushed out of the chair. "I think I'll go for a walk. Maybe I'll go into town and browse around. I have a lot of thinking to do."

She nodded, and he turned and climbed

slowly down the stairs. His shoulders that usually looked so square and strong sloped slightly now under the weight of all his problems. Her heart clutched at the pain he was going through. But he was doing exactly what Mom wanted. What she said she needed. So that was probably a good thing, wasn't it?

Maybe.

Maybe not.

Because if they weren't living together, how would they find the time to talk? To sort it all out?

She chastised herself for not realizing how miserable her mom was. Well, she knew her mom had been struggling a bit, but she thought it was just adjusting to the whole empty nest thing. And to be honest, she'd been so busy with her own job, she hadn't really spent enough time with her mom to catch on that things were so rough for her. Maybe if she'd spent more time with her, gone over to the house more often, done *something*... Maybe all this wouldn't be happening.

But maybe her parents would still work everything out.

Or what if it had gone on so long that her mother had hardened her heart from the pain she'd been feeling and it was all too late? Fear sliced through her that this was exactly what had happened and nothing could fix it.

CHAPTER 16

I t was barely light when Frankie headed out for her now regular beach walk. She needed time to think and wasn't ready to speak to anyone yet. She wasn't up to talking to Will this morning. And this would be a good way to give him his space. Of course, soon he'd have all the space he needed with his own condo.

She'd be living alone in the house they'd shared for so long. Just like she wanted. That was what she wanted, right?

He said he'd change, that things would be different, but would they? Could they change? Hadn't they drifted too far apart by now? Her heart was frozen now, a needed protection from the hurt she'd been feeling for so long. She wasn't sure there was any way to change that. Or if she wanted to, because what if she let him back in and then they drifted apart again? If she became invisible again?

She walked way down the beach—farther than her usual walk—then suddenly she spun around and headed back to the cottages. She knew what she needed to do now. She needed to talk to Rose. Even though she'd only known Rose for a few days, the woman always had a way of helping to sort things out for her.

She picked up her pace, hoping Rose would still be out at her usual spot. As she got near, she spotted Rose and relief swept through her. She trotted up to her and dropped down on the sand. "I was looking for you."

"And here I am." Rose's face lit up with a smile.

"I… I need to talk. Do you have time?"

"Of course."

"So much has happened since yesterday when we talked. Yesterday when I got back from shopping with the girls…" She stopped for a moment, catching her breath. "When I got back, Will told me he'd rented a condo, and he's moving out next week."

"He did that after you talked to him and told him how you felt?" Rose's eyes widened in surprise.

"No… not exactly. I was going to talk to him after this vacation was over. But then he went and rented a place. And he was so proud that he'd finally done what I'd asked him to." She picked up a small piece of driftwood and ran her finger along the smooth edge. "He's… so hurt. I can see it in his eyes."

"Then you should talk to him, shouldn't you?"

"But he finally did what I've been asking him to do for months."

Rose reached out and touched her arm. "But is that really what you want? Or do you just need things to change? Change somehow? Because you can no longer keep going on like you two have been, can you?"

"No, we can't live like we have been. The tension. The looks he gives me. The hurt in his eyes. And yet, even the hurt look in his eyes doesn't seem to melt my heart toward him."

"Do you want to stay married to him?" Rose looked directly at her.

"I… I can't really imagine my life without

him. But I don't want to live with him the way things are. I can't. I can't stay invisible any longer."

"You need to tell him all of that before he moves out. And I'm thinking your idea to wait to talk to him until after vacation was just avoidance. Avoidance of doing a hard thing."

She closed her eyes. "You're right. I should have talked to him yesterday. Not put it off. Because if things are going to change, we do have to talk. I know that. I was just so shocked when he said he was moving out." She closed her eyes.

"Doing what you asked him to do," Rose said quietly.

"Yes, but after talking to you yesterday, I thought maybe we could..." She shook her head. "I don't know. I don't know anything anymore." A tear trailed down her cheek, and she dashed it away. "I feel like a yo-yo with my emotions and my thoughts. Now he's acting all distant and giving me the space I wanted and it's all so messed up."

"Talk to him."

"But he *finally* listened to me. He never truly listens to me. And now he did what I wanted. I'd look like a fool if I then ask him to talk. I think I should just let him move out. Give us both space. Then maybe after a while, we can talk."

"So you're going to let your pride stand in your way? You don't want to look foolish?" Rose's eyebrows lifted. "I still think you should put that aside and talk to him."

"And tell him what?"

"Explain how you feel like he's ignored you. Doesn't want you, like you explained to me yesterday. How you feel lost now with him busy at work and the girls moved out."

"But he knows all that."

"Does he?" Rose tilted her head. "Sometimes we think someone knows something, but... they don't."

"He's going to think I'm crazy. I insisted he move out. He finally *actually* listened to me. He gets an apartment, doing exactly what I asked. And now... I just don't know." She dashed away another tear. "And it gets worse. The girls found out. They saw we were sleeping in separate rooms and then asked us directly what was wrong. I couldn't lie to them."

"No, I don't suppose you could."

"Now they are so upset. And get this.

They've planned a surprise anniversary party for Will and me. Invited a bunch of our friends. I mean, can things get any worse?"

"I think it's time you found Will and talked to him. See what you two really want to do. Whether it's stay together, or him move out, at least the two of you should discuss it and listen to each other. Really listen to what the other person is saying."

"I know you're right. I'm just... just a bit afraid of doing it. Because what if we talk and can't work it out? Then... then everything is just... over."

"You won't know until you talk to him."

She pushed off the sand and stood. "You're right. I'm going to go find him right now. Because if I wait any longer, I'll just think of a reason why it's the wrong time."

CHAPTER 17

W ill walked toward town, mindlessly wandering down streets until he hit Magnolia. He popped into Sea Glass Cafe and ordered breakfast. Sitting there all alone just reminded him that he'd be eating all his meals alone when he moved out.

Not that he was much of a cook. He'd probably be ordering takeout. How had it all just fallen apart for him at this stage of life?

At this stage, he was supposed to be thinking about retirement and more time to spend with his family. He'd actually thought they'd have a few grandkids by now that he could spoil. Nothing had turned out the way he thought it would.

He paid for his breakfast and walked outside, feeling lost. The sun shone down on the sidewalk with a golden glow. But even the sunshine didn't raise his spirits.

He glanced up and down the street, trying to decide what to do next. He couldn't bear to head back to the cottage and see Frankie. There wasn't really anything else to say. He'd done what she asked. They just needed to get through the next few days—and the anniversary party— then head home and go their separate ways.

The anniversary party. That would be interesting. All their friends there. He and Frankie pretending everything was just great. He glanced down the street and saw Daisy. She saw him and hurried down the sidewalk toward him.

"There you are. I was just getting ready to call you. I found the lilacs. They'll be here tomorrow and I'll get them ready for you."

A wide smile crept across his face, and for the first time in days, a tiny light broke through the clouds of his life. "That's wonderful." He gave Daisy a hug. "Just great."

She laughed as she stepped back out of his

hug. "Well, I do like to make my customers happy."

"You really did."

"And one more thing. When you said you were looking for a small gift for your wife. I saw this in Beachside Bookshop. Collette—she's the owner—she sells small bouquets of my flowers in her shop. Anyway, I saw this at her shop and thought of you. Well, thought of your wife." Daisy held out her phone with a photo on it. A bracelet of lilac-colored beads rested on a bed of silk. "I know you said your wife loved lilacs. These are lavender jade."

"She does, and it's her favorite color, too. And what synchronicity. You might not believe this, but I got a similar bracelet for her for a wedding gift."

"So you like it?"

He handed back her phone. "It's perfect." He laughed out loud and couldn't help himself. He scooped Daisy up in another hug. "You have really made my day. My week. I'll have lilacs for her and she'll love this bracelet."

She beamed. "Good. Collette said she'd hold it for you. I just had a feeling about it."

"Daisy, you are just the best."

"Glad I could help you out. I hope you have a lovely anniversary. The shop is just down the street if you want to go pick it up."

"I do. It's perfect. I can't thank you enough. And I found out the girls are throwing us a surprise anniversary party on Saturday."

"Ah, you found out." Daisy grinned. "I'm doing the flowers for your party, too. I heard it was a secret."

"Well it was a secret, but now it's not. And you're doing the flowers for it?" He laughed. Small world.

"Yes, your daughter, Katie, arranged it."

Of course she did. Katie thought of everything.

"I can drop off the lilacs when I bring the other flowers if you'd like."

"That would be perfect." He reached out and squeezed Daisy's hand. "I can't thank you enough."

She smiled up at him. "I'm so glad it's all working out for you."

He watched as Daisy hurried back down the street. He wouldn't exactly say everything was working out. But at least he'd have Frankie's favorite flowers for their anniversary. And the bracelet wasn't a big showy gift, just a tiny reminder of their wedding.

Hopefully, Frankie would be pleased, not mad. But then, who knew with Frankie these days?

Frankie ran into Violet, who told her she'd seen Will and he said he was headed to town, so Frankie did the same. She was going to track him down. Talk to him. They had to talk. It might not change anything, but it was a start.

She hurried down the sidewalk and headed toward Magnolia. Maybe Will would be shopping there. If not on Magnolia, she'd find him no matter where he was, even if it took her all day.

A seed of hope grew inside her. At least they should try. Talk things out.

She turned the corner and spied Will across the street, barely a block away. Perfect. She stepped out on the sidewalk and paused as a woman came hurrying up to him. To her utter surprise, they talked for a moment, then Will hugged her, a huge smile on his face. Stunned, Frankie took a step back. Who was this woman?

She glanced around and stepped back into an entrance to a shop—yes, hiding from Will— and watched him and the woman. She was pretty. Petite with blonde hair that bounced around her shoulders. An engaging smile.

The woman handed Will something, and he looked at it and his laugh rang across the distance... and he *hugged* the woman again. And Will wasn't much of a hugger. What in the world was going on?

Was Will seeing someone? Had he met someone here in Moonbeam? He certainly had been using the excuse he was running errands enough this week. Or was this woman someone he knew from somewhere else? Who just happened to be here? That didn't make sense.

Her heart skittered in her chest. Maybe the woman had come to Moonbeam to be with Will. Maybe he'd been seeing the woman for a while and that was why he was so distant with her.

Maybe he'd met this new woman, and that was what finally made him decide to go rent the condo. Maybe it wasn't that he was listening to her after all.

So many maybes.

Will reached out and took the woman's hand.

She'd seen enough. She gulped a breath, spun around, and hurried around the corner, unable to watch her husband with this woman one minute longer.

Fine. Just fine. If someone new had caught his eye, if this was going to be their new normal... It was just fine if a skinny, pretty blonde was what he wanted.

She hurried down the sidewalk, her heart squeezing in her chest, her breath coming out in ragged gasps. What had she thought would happen? She'd been pushing Will away for months and months. Telling him she needed space. To move out.

Well, it looked like he was not only moving out but moving on.

She reached her cottage and flung open the door, closing it behind her and leaning against it. Her whole world spun out of control. And here she was, planning on talking to Will. To see if he would stay and they'd work things out.

But he was holding the hand of another woman. She couldn't quite reconcile with that, and it burned her with the fury of a violent storm.

She looked around the room in a panic, searching for her purse and the car keys. Finding them, she raced back out the door and jumped into the car. It ground to life, and she pulled out of the drive, the crushed shells spraying out behind her.

She sped away from Moonbeam. From Will. Will who looked at that woman with such delight. Such happiness. She couldn't deny it or make excuses for it. Then he'd taken the woman's hand. Right there out in the open for everyone to see.

A thought she never believed she would have whirled around in her mind. Her husband was cheating on her. Or was planning to. Whichever it was, he'd been absolutely delighted to see the woman.

She had to get away, and the only place she could think to go was home. Back to the safety of her home.

The one she'd live in alone as soon as Will moved out.

And the day he moved out couldn't come any too soon for her.

CHAPTER 18

Melody looked up mid-morning from pouring a cup of coffee for one of her customers right as Violet stepped into the cafe. "Be with you in a sec. Just grab a table anywhere."

She finished with her customer and crossed over to where Violet was slipping into a seat. Violet laughed. "I couldn't wait any longer. I'm dying to hear how your date went. Got time to join me?"

Melody glanced around the cafe at the few remaining customers. "Sure, just let me get this one table's tab run, and I'll be back. Want some coffee?"

"Sounds great."

She returned with two cups of coffee and sank into the chair across from Violet, scooting one mug across the table.

"So, tell me. How did it go?"

"It was… I don't know… awkward at first. But then Ethan admitted he was nervous and it kind of broke the ice for us. After that, I relaxed and had a good time."

"A good time, or a great time?" Violet cocked her head.

"Okay, it bordered on a great time. I thought I'd feel strange dating someone after all this time. But Ethan put me at ease. We ate at The Cabot Hotel, then went out to the pavilion. It was a beautiful night of moonlight and stars."

"Are you going to go out again?"

"Yes, we're going on a picnic on Sunday."

Violet leaned forward. "Incoming. Here come the twins."

Jackie and Jillian Jenkins hurried over to them. "Good morning. Melody, we heard you had a date with Ethan Chambers last night."

Of course they did. The twins knew everything that went on in town. "I went to dinner with Ethan, yes."

Jackie's eyes lit up. "See, I knew it. I've

known for a long time that Ethan had eyes for you."

"We just weren't sure why it took him so long to ask you out." Jillian shook her head. "But we're glad he finally did."

Yet more people who'd caught on that Ethan was interested in going out with her. How had she missed it for so long? She just smiled at the twins, not giving them any more fuel for gossip.

"And was it magical?" Jackie asked in a hushed voice, unwilling to let the questions end.

"I'm not sure I'd call it magical…"

"Oh, but first dates are so much fun, aren't they? Getting to know a person. I'm so happy for you." Jillian's face broke into a wide smile.

Evelyn came out of the kitchen just then. "Oh, Jackie, Jillian, go grab a table and let me get some menus."

As the women walked away, Melody mouthed thank you.

Evelyn leaned over and whispered, "You're welcome. You looked like you needed a bit of a rescue. I've got this. You have your coffee with Violet."

Melody turned back to her friend. "You

know, they're probably going to tell a billion people about my date."

Violet grinned. "At least. The whole town will know by nightfall."

She looked over at the twins. "They mean well, but I just don't like everyone to know my business. Especially since this is all so new to me."

"I'm not sure anyone has ever found a way to thwart the Jenkins twins."

She let out a sigh. "No, I don't suppose they have."

"Anyway, forget about the twins. Tell me more about your night. I swear I won't spread it all over town."

"Well, we talked a lot. It was... easy to be with him. Nice. Then he drove me home and asked if I'd go out with him again. That's when we decided to go on a picnic on Sunday."

"That sounds fun."

"He held my hand. It was strange at first, but then I kind of liked it. And..." She paused as the heat of a blush crept across her cheeks. She leaned forward across the table and whispered, "And as he was leaving, he said... He said he was going to kiss me, but chickened out."

Violet laughed. "You two are quite the pair, aren't you? Did you want him to kiss you?"

"Isn't that the question I'd like an answer to? I just don't know…"

CHAPTER 19

Frankie pulled the car into the garage and punched the remote to close the door behind her. It lumbered down the track and settled with a thump. She went inside and stalked around her house, slamming doors and fuming.

After yet another slammed door, she finally went and grabbed some boxes from the garage and took them into the guest room where Will was staying. She opened his dresser, noticing his socks were in one big pile, not neatly paired like when she did his laundry. His boxers were in another pile, not folded nicely like they should be. She guessed that's what happened when she quit doing his laundry for him. But that wasn't her problem, was it? She scooped all of them out and dumped them into the first box. Then she went into the bathroom and cleared out every single item of his, shoving all it in another box.

She opened the closet and stared at his clothes hanging there in disarray. Not organized like she'd always done for him, with work shirts all together next to his dress slacks, knit shirts next to casual pants. Just crammed in there willy-nilly. That would be his life now. Doing his own laundry and just shoving stuff in drawers and closets.

Unless, of course, this new woman took over the laundry. Well, she could have it. Have him. Her pulse thundered through her.

She yanked out the clothes and dumped them into two huge boxes, then tugged and pushed and dragged the boxes to the garage. Stripped the bed and threw the sheets in the laundry. Cleaned every single surface of the bedroom and bathroom. Soon, every bit of Will was erased.

Her breath came out in gasps from the

exertion, but still, all the hard work hadn't managed to dampen her anger. Anger at Will. At herself.

When she'd felt invisible, she'd been right. This new blonde certainly wasn't invisible with her bubbly laugh, cute hair, and ridiculously fit body.

She glanced at the mirror and growled. "Look at you, woman. Your hair is a mess. You've put on way too many pounds. No wonder he went looking for someone else." Bitterness raged through her and mixed with disappointment. Disappointment with Will, with herself.

She whirled around and marched into the bedroom, eyeing it carefully to see if there were any more reminders of Will. She walked over to the dresser and picked up a framed photo— probably ten years old—of her and Will all dressed up for a Christmas party. In the picture, she had on a red dress at least two sizes smaller than what she wore now. She stared at it, barely recognizing the two of them. Were they happy then? She couldn't even remember. When had all this started? The distance between them?

She couldn't stand looking at the photo for one more moment and went over and dropped it into the trashcan. The glass shattered, just like their lives.

She jerked open each drawer to make sure nothing was left of his clothes. Then the chair in the corner he loved so much mocked her. She tugged it out into the hall, scratching the floor in the process. More anger surged through her. Just great. His final blow could be a gouge in their floor that she'd see every single day. She carefully carted it out to the garage so it wouldn't mark up the floor or walls, sweat rolling down her face at the effort. She shoved it against the garage wall with her foot and swept her damp hair away from her face with an aggravated shove. He could take it or she'd put it out in the trash.

She stomped back inside and grabbed a glass from the cabinet, which she filled with cool water and pressed against her forehead. Then she drained the glass, staring out the window at the backyard. It was a good thing she'd hired a yard service when Will had gotten so busy with his job because she sure wasn't going to mow this yard.

She turned around and leaned against the counter. And really, what did she need with a house this big? Four bedrooms and it would just be her now. Maybe she'd sell the thing and find some cute little place all her own. She closed her eyes against the memory of the girls sitting at the kitchen table, their little legs swinging as they worked on their homework. The drawings and starred papers from school hanging on the fridge. Or the memory of them when they were a bit older, sitting at the table laughing about something that had happened at school. So many memories.

She scrubbed her hands over her face, but it did little to erase the memories, the sounds of their laughter. How could she leave the house she raised the girls in? It was still their home, even if they'd moved out on their own.

Only it didn't feel like *her* home anymore. It felt like a massive cave of pain and loss, suffocating her.

She crossed over and sat in a chair, burying her face in her hands as hot tears flowed down her cheeks and over her hands. How had she gotten to this point in her life? Life was never supposed to be like this. This is not what she'd planned for this stage of her life.

Will got back to the cottage and hid the present in a stack of t-shirts, pleased he'd actually packed enough shirts without Frankie's prompting. There was no sign of Frankie, so he grabbed a book and went out to relax and read on the porch. At least he still had these few days with her. Then, after he moved out like she wanted and gave her some time on her own, he was determined to convince her they should talk. Maybe go out on a date. He was determined to do anything and everything to try to get them back on track and woo her back.

Katie crossed over from her cottage and joined him. "You doing okay?"

"I'm fine, Katydid. Don't worry about me."

"But I do worry. About you and Mom."

"Do you know where she is? She wasn't here when I got back from town."

"No, I haven't seen her. Surely she isn't still out beach walking for this long."

"No, that would be a long walk, even for your mother."

Violet came out of the office and waved to them. She jogged across the courtyard. "How's everything going? Do you need anything?"

"No, everything is fine," Katie said. "Oh, and the surprise is off on the anniversary party. Mom and Dad found out. So we don't have to sneak around or make up excuses while we're getting everything ready on Saturday."

Violet smiled. "Well, that will make it easier, but sorry about the surprise."

"No, it's fine." Will was actually glad they'd found out. He wasn't big on surprises, and he felt like he'd had enough of them with Frankie this year.

"Say, have you seen Mom around?" Katie asked.

"I saw her leave in the car a while ago."

Will frowned. "Hm, she didn't mention running any errands. Well, maybe she thought of something she needed for the party."

Violet turned, popped down the stairs, and gave a small wave. "Let me know if you need anything. Can't wait to get the courtyard all set up for your party."

"I wonder where Mom went." Katie frowned as she took out her phone. "I'm going to text her." She sent off the text, then stared at the screen.

"No response?"

"No, but you know how Mom is with texts. She'll see it eventually and answer." She set the phone down on the table next to her.

"We really do appreciate you girls planning this party. It was very thoughtful. I'm sorry about the timing of you finding out about our separation."

"It's probably best to still have the party. Otherwise, gossip will run wild. This way you and Mom can control when people find out about... about your... uh... living apart."

Will reached over and patted her knee. "Don't worry, Katydid."

Her phone vibrated on the table and dinged with an incoming text. "Hey, it's Mom. She's..." Katie looked up at him. "She's back at home."

"Back home? Why?"

"I don't know. Let me find out."

Mom? When are you coming back?

I'm not.

Not coming to the anniversary party?

I am not. Sorry.

What's wrong?

Nothing to be concerned about. Sorry for all the trouble you went to with the party. I'm turning my phone off now. I need time alone.

Katie set her phone down. "She says she's not coming back here."

"But why? What about the family vacation? The party?"

"She's not coming."

He frowned. "I don't understand. She was in favor of still having it so everyone wouldn't find out about us just yet."

"I don't know."

He stood up, his heart thumping. *Now* what was going on with Frankie? "I should go talk to her."

Katie stood and put her hand on his arm. "No, Dad. I think it might be better if I go talk to her."

He let out a long sigh. "Maybe you're right. If something upset her enough that she left, she might not even speak to me. But she'd never turn you away."

"I'll go right away. I'll call after I find out what's going on."

CHAPTER 20

K atie grabbed her purse, scribbled a note to Stacey, and hurried out to her car. She pulled away from Moonbeam and headed toward home.

What could have happened that changed her mother's mind? She'd been all fine with still having the party. Would they have to call everyone at the last minute and cancel? She shuddered at the chaos that would ensue from all those calls and explaining why the party was canceled.

Stacey would help her make all those calls, wouldn't she?

Probably not.

But she certainly didn't want to make all those calls without speaking to her mom first and finding out what was going on.

She finally pulled into the driveway of her childhood home after what seemed like the longest drive ever. She stepped out of the car and glanced up at the house for a moment while a pang of nostalgia mixed with dread filled her.

Would it still feel the same coming here if her parents separated? They wouldn't have family dinners here anymore. Or holidays. Or last-minute barbecues. So much would change.

She stared at the house, taking in every little detail. The swing on the front porch. The worn wooden front steps. The flower bed lining the front of the house that her mother kept carefully tended. She still felt like this was *her* house, no matter that she was grown and didn't live here anymore. The house she grew up in. The house she loved. With a shake of her head to clear her thoughts, she hurried up the stairs and inside.

"Mom? You here?"

Her mother walked out of the kitchen, a polishing cloth in one hand, a silver bowl in the other. That wasn't good. Her mother polished silver when she was very, very upset.

"What are you doing here?" Her mother eyed her suspiciously.

"I came to check on you. I was worried. You just up and disappeared without a word."

"I'm sorry about that. Didn't mean to worry you. I just needed to be… away."

"Dad's worried, too. He was going to come talk to you, but I said maybe I should instead."

"Good plan. I don't want to see him." She turned around and walked back into the kitchen.

Katie trailed behind her. Silver platters and bowls lay scattered on the counter. It looked like a collection of every single piece of silver in the house. This was so not a good sign at all.

"Mom, what's wrong? I thought we were going ahead with the party. Did you decide it would be too hard? We'll do whatever you want."

"There's no way I could ever be at that anniversary party with your father."

She frowned. "But why not? What changed?"

"Katie, it's really something that's between your father and me."

"But Mom, he has no clue why you left."

She gave a little laugh. "Oh, I bet if he thinks on it, he could figure it out."

"You're not making any sense, and I swear, I saw his face. He had no idea why you left."

"Oh, he does. He just doesn't know he's been caught yet."

She walked over to her mom and took her arm, turning her around. "Mom, please tell me what's going on."

Her mother closed her eyes for a moment, pain clearly etched across her features. "It's just… well, you'll find out soon enough. I saw your father… I saw him with another woman."

Katie gasped. "No, you didn't."

She nodded. "Yes, I did. In Moonbeam. I don't know if she came to Moonbeam to meet up with him, or what. Maybe that's why he was always off *running errands*. But I saw them both with my own two eyes."

"Are you sure?"

"He hugged her. He held her hand. And the look of pure delight on his face when he talked to her. I couldn't miss that." She turned back to the sink and picked up a silver tray, smeared on some silver polish, and rubbed vigorously.

"Oh, Mom. I don't know what to say." Her heart plummeted. It's exactly what she'd been afraid of. That maybe one of them had cheated on the other. But she still couldn't picture her father cheating on her mom.

"Katie, I saw him. There's just no denying it. Earlier today I'd thought... Well, it was silly, but I'd thought maybe I'd ask him to wait to move out. I've been trying to protect my heart from any more hurt and disappointment, but then I decided to maybe give it one more chance. I decided I was willing to risk getting hurt again if things didn't work out. That maybe we should sit down and really talk. I'd promised myself I wouldn't walk away like I usually do when the conversation gets heated. But now?" She shrugged. "Now there's no point. Your father has moved on."

She draped an arm around her mother's shoulders. "Oh, Mom. I'm sorry. And to find out like that. To actually see him."

"Katie, you're sweet for coming and checking on me, but now I need to be alone. I need time to process all this. And ask your father to let me know when he's moving, and I'll make sure I'm out of the house when he gets his things."

Everything sounded so final. So hopeless. She kissed her mom's cheek. "I'll make sure you know when he'll be here. Mom, I'm so sorry. Are you sure you want to be alone? I can stay." A strong surge of protectiveness swept through her. She'd do anything and everything to help her mother through this. Her father cheated. Cheated!

"I'm positive. I just… I just need time." At least the anger in her mother's eyes had chased away the sadness that had been there. Her mom picked up another piece of silver.

"If you're sure." Katie turned and headed out to her car, her jaw clenched, anger burning through her. How dare Dad sit there this morning looking confused about why Mom had left? Did he think he could keep his affair a secret?

And here she'd been feeling sorry for him.

She climbed into her car, and even the comfort of her beloved Tesla did nothing to soothe her nerves. The car silently started, and she headed back toward Moonbeam and the cottages.

Her thoughts raced as quickly as the car... not that she went even one mile over the speed limit. She never did. She was a very careful driver. But as each mile slipped past, her anger grew to a boiling fury.

CHAPTER 21

W ill stared at the unknown caller notification coming up on his phone. He didn't have time for spam calls. He needed to hear from Katie and find out what was going on with Frankie.

He declined the incoming call and got up and paced the porch. Back and forth. One plank squeaked every time he got to it, and he considered going over to the office and asking Violet for a hammer so he could fix it so it would quit annoying him.

Though just about everything annoyed him right now.

The squeaky porch. The fact that the breeze

had died down and it was getting hot. And of course the big one… the fact that Frankie had just up and left without a word. She'd surprised him a lot this year, but today's surprise was the biggest.

He spun on his heels and changed direction.

The phone rang again. Unknown caller. Annoyed, he answered it this time, ready to give whoever was at the other end of the line a piece of his mind.

"Mr. Winters?"

"Yes, who's this?" he said brusquely, hoping to give the caller a clue he was busy.

"It's the emergency room at South Florida General Hospital. Your daughter Katie is here and asked us to call you."

"Katie? Why is she there?"

"She's been in a car accident."

His heart double-timed in his chest, his thoughts running wild with all the horrible possibilities. "Is she okay?"

"The doctor is checking her out now."

He racked his brain, trying to remember seeing that hospital. "I don't know where South Florida General is." He couldn't disguise the panic in his voice. He twirled around to head inside to grab his keys but then remembered Frankie had taken the car.

"It's just over the bridge from Belle Island. On the mainland. First Street and Island Road."

First Street and Island Road. First Street and Island Road. He imprinted the address in his mind. "Tell her I'll be there as soon as I can."

He grabbed his wallet and ran over to the girls' cottage to tell Stacey what had happened, but no one answered. He'd have to text her when he had a minute. He raced toward the office and burst inside. "Violet, I need help."

She looked up from behind the reception desk. "What's wrong?"

"Katie's been in an accident. She's at the hospital. South Florida General. But I don't have a car."

"Hold on, I'll get my keys. And I'll get Aspen to cover the desk. Within minutes, they were headed to Violet's car as Aspen jogged over to the office and waved them on.

"I've got this," she called out.

"You know where this hospital is? They said

on the mainland across from Belle Island. First Street and Island Road."

"Yes, I know where it is. Won't take long."

Frankie. He had to tell Frankie. He pulled out his phone and called, but she didn't pick up. *For Pete's sake, Francine. Pick up.*

He called Stacey, and she didn't answer. Great. He tried Frankie again. No answer. Maybe she was just ignoring his calls. He texted both of them saying to contact him immediately. It was an emergency.

Surely Frankie would call when she saw that. He didn't want to leave a message that Katie had been in an accident. Especially since he didn't know how she was. He clenched his teeth. She'd be okay. She would.

Stacey called in a few minutes and he told her what had happened. "I'll call as soon as I know how she is. Can you try getting a hold of your mother? She's... ah... she's back at home. But she's not answering my calls or texts."

"She's at home? I don't understand."

"I don't either. But just try to reach her."

"I will. But call me as soon as you know anything."

"Okay, I will."

Within twenty minutes—which seemed like hours—he was rushing into the emergency room. "I'm Mr. Winters. My daughter is here."

"She's been taken for x-rays. I'll come get you as soon as she's back."

"She's okay, though?"

"I'll get the doctor to come talk to you."

He wanted to scream out his frustration. Violet walked into the waiting room and over to him, placing her hand on his arm. "Here, let's sit. I'm sure the doctor will be out soon."

"You don't have to stay. I know you're busy."

"No, Aspen has the desk. I'll just sit here with you for a bit." Concern filled her eyes.

"I just…" He raked his hands through his hair. "She has to be okay. I shouldn't have let her go back to Sarasota."

Violet didn't ask why Katie had headed home, and he didn't offer up an explanation. He checked his phone, but no message or text from Frankie.

For crying out loud… Why wasn't she answering her phone? He texted her again.

He sank onto the hard waiting room chair

and drummed his fingers on the armrest. The minutes ticked away on the large clock on the wall. The clock was askew, and he thought about standing on a chair to fix it because it annoyed him. Didn't anyone who worked here notice the clock was cockeyed?

He didn't know why he was taking his anger out on the workers here in the ER. He was mad at himself. He never should have let Katie go back home. This was his mess to clean up, not hers.

If *he'd* gone home, then she wouldn't have been in an accident.

What had Frankie told her? Was Katie so upset she shouldn't have been driving? Any way he looked at it, he knew one thing was true. This was all his fault.

Frankie slowly picked up another silver tray. Pretty soon she'd have all the silver polished, then what would she do? Usually polishing the silver would soothe her anger, but it wasn't working this time. Not at all.

After she finished polishing the last piece,

she crossed to the fridge. Did it need cleaning? It probably did. She had a sudden urge to clean everything. She started to pull out random food and set it on the counter.

A knock came at the back door and she wanted to ignore it. She glanced out the window to make sure it wasn't Will. But it was just their neighbor, Adele.

She didn't really want to talk to her either, but Adele had probably seen her pull in. She saw everything going on in the neighborhood. She sighed and crossed over to answer the door.

"Hi, Adele."

"Oh, you are here. Stacey called me to come over and see if you were. She said you aren't answering your phone."

She didn't really want to talk to Stacey, either. She wasn't ready to rehash all of this with her.

"I turned off my phone for a bit."

"Well, Stacey said there's an emergency. Something about Katie. Wants you to call."

Her pulse galloped as she rushed over to her purse and tugged out her phone. So many missed calls and texts.

"Ah, thanks, Adele. I'll call her now." She

closed the door on Adele, ignoring her startled expression, and tapped on the phone to call Stacey.

"Mom, thank goodness."

"What happened? What's wrong? Is Katie okay?"

"I'm not sure. All I know is she's in the hospital. Some kind of accident. But Dad hasn't called with an update. She's at South Florida General."

She grabbed her keys off the table and dashed out the door, ignoring the open fridge and all the food out on the counter. She hurried into the garage, juggling her purse, keys, and phone. "Where is that hospital?"

"Near Belle Island. I'll look up the address and text it to you."

"Thanks."

"Why weren't you answering the phone?"

"I... I didn't hear it. I turned it off." Guilt swept through her. She'd ignored her phone right when Katie needed her.

"Call me as soon as you find out anything."

She pulled out of the garage, her mind racing. Had Katie been so upset when she left that it affected her driving? She should have let Katie stay with her, like she offered.

Maybe Katie just needed some time, too. But no, she'd sent her back to face Will because she couldn't face him herself.

This was all her fault.

CHAPTER 22

Frankie rushed into the emergency room, looking around wildly for a sign of Katie. She saw Will and Violet sitting across the room.

Will stood. "Frankie, you're here. Finally."

She rushed over to them. "Katie, where is she? How is she?"

He pulled her into his arms, and she briefly wanted to take solace there, but she jerked back out of his arms. She didn't need anything from him. Nothing at all.

He looked at her for a moment and shook his head. "I'm waiting to hear from the doctor."

"Why aren't you back there with her?"

"They took her for some tests."

"Well, I can't just sit here while she's in here

somewhere all alone." She spun around to talk to the woman at the reception desk. "I need to see my daughter. Katie Winters."

"The doctor is coming out momentarily to speak with you."

"But I want to see her now." Despair and panic raced through her. Was she okay? Why wouldn't anyone tell them anything? Didn't they understand her daughter was hurt? Katie needed her.

A woman in a white coat walked out from the back. "I'm Dr. Harden. Are you Katie's family?"

"Yes." Will stepped up beside her and put his arm around her shoulder.

She stepped sideways, out of his arm. "Yes, I'm her mother. Is she okay?"

"She will be. She'll be bruised from the seatbelt, but there's nothing broken. We took x-rays as a precaution. She does have a cut on her forehead, but it's all cleaned up and she didn't need stitches. She was very lucky."

Relief swept through her, followed immediately by tears. Will started to reach for her but dropped his hands to his side. He was clearly fighting back his own tears. She swiped at the tears. "Can we see her?"

"Yes, come on back."

They followed Dr. Harden back through the maze of hallways until she stopped by a room. "Katie is in there. I'll get the paperwork ready for her discharge."

"Thank you so much, Dr. Harden. I appreciate you taking care of her."

Dr. Harden smiled and disappeared down the hall.

Will looked at her. "You ready?"

She ignored him and pushed through the door. Katie sat in bed looking… annoyed.

"Katie." She rushed over and threw her arms around her daughter, pulling her close.

"Mom, I'm fine. Really."

She stepped back and ran her gaze all over her daughter, taking in everything. A small bandage peeked out near her hairline. "Are you sure? Are you in pain?"

"Just a little sore."

"What happened?"

"Some kid ran a stop sign. Hit my car. You should have seen how scared he was. He'd only had his license for a week."

"Sounds like he needs more driving lessons." Will walked up beside the bed.

"I should have never let you drive back here. I should have let you stay with me."

"Mom, it was just an accident. The boy wasn't hurt, thank goodness. And Dr. Harden said I'll be fine."

Will stepped closer and hugged Katie. Katie accepted the hug for a moment, then pulled back and looked at her, then him, a guilty look on her face as if she was betraying her by hugging her father.

"I was so worried about you, Katydid. You shouldn't scare us like that." Will stood by the side of the bed. She willed him to move away, but he remained.

Katie winced and touched the bandage on her forehead. "Well, I sure didn't do it on purpose. I wouldn't have minded skipping this part, either. And my car. It's got quite the bash in the side. They towed it away."

"It's metal and money, Katydid. You'll get it fixed. We're just grateful you weren't hurt. I'll make some calls for you and deal with it."

"You don't have to do that."

"I want to. You should take it easy."

"I'll handle it, Dad." Katie's words came out sharply, and Will's forehead wrinkled with a frown.

Dr. Harden popped into the room. "Okay, you're all set to leave. Just check out at the desk when you're ready."

"Hey, doc, could you tell my parents that I'm just fine?"

"She really is fine. But it's never wrong to spoil a person after they've been in an accident." She smiled as she left the room.

"You two go on out to the waiting room. I'll get dressed and we'll get out of here. I want to go back to the cottages."

"Wouldn't you rather come home for a few days? Take it easy?" Surely Katie would be more comfortable at home in her own room.

"No, I'm fine. I'd rather spend the rest of the week in Moonbeam at the beach. Are you going to go back home, Mom?" Katie looked at her expectantly. "It's okay if you want to."

"I... uh..." She looked at Will, then Katie. "Of course I'm going to Moonbeam. I need to be there to take care of you."

"Mom, you heard Dr. Harden. I'm okay, really."

The doctor did say she was fine, but she couldn't bear to leave and go back home. She wanted to stay with Katie. Keep an eye on her. Pamper her. Make sure she was safe and taken care of. She couldn't leave that up to Will. Didn't trust him to do that. Didn't trust him about anything.

"Come on, Frankie. Let's let her get dressed, then we'll head back."

She slipped past Will without a word, but what she wanted to do was to tell him not to tell her what to do. Ever. He had no right. None at all.

Will started to help Katie settle into the front seat of the car, but she pulled her arm from him and he swore he saw a look of anger—and maybe disgust—in her eyes. What was that about? Were all the Winter women suddenly mad at him? "Katie?"

"I've got it," she said a bit sharply as she slid into the seat.

He turned and reached for the keys from Frankie.

"No, I'm driving." She faced him defiantly.

He held up both hands in defeat, then slipped into the back seat. Frankie always let him drive. Seemed to prefer it. But not today.

Frankie eased the car out of the hospital parking lot and onto First Street. Katie laughed. "Mom, just drive. I'm fine."

"I just want to make sure you're comfortable."

Frankie drove slowly down the street, slowing down way before each stop sign, making sure they rolled to a gentle stop. Katie kept her gaze to the front of the car, never looking back at him.

"You sure you're okay, Katie?" He leaned forward in his seat and touched her shoulder.

She pushed his hand away. "I'm just great."

There was that sharpness in her tone again. Now what had he done? Was Katie mad at him, too? Maybe for allowing her to go back home and then this accident happened? He never should have let her go.

"Do you want me to stop and get you anything special to eat? Are you hungry? In pain?" Frankie glanced over at Katie.

"Not in pain. Just a bit sore. You're going to

drive me nuts if you hover over me for the rest of our trip."

They rode the rest of the way back to Moonbeam with Frankie anxiously glancing over at Katie as if she would disappear. He didn't blame her for that. He spent most of the ride staring at Katie, too. Grateful she was going to be okay. But no one spoke. The tension between all of them crackled through the air, threatening to burst the car wide open and send them all hurtling in different directions.

Frankie finally turned into the parking space near the cottages. Stacey came flying out of her cottage and yanked open Katie's door. "Are you okay? And what happened to everyone saying they'd call me?"

Guilt surged through Will. He had promised to call Stacey but forgot in all the confusion. He stepped out of the car. "Sorry, I should have."

"Are you okay?" Stacey reached out a hand, and Katie took it and slid out of the car. Stacey hugged her. "Oh, my gosh, I was so worried."

"I'm okay."

Stacey stepped back. "Are you? You sure? And where's your car?"

"It got towed. Had some damage."

Stacey turned to Frankie. "Mom, why were you back home? And why was Katie there? And why doesn't anyone ever tell me anything?"

Frankie stepped around the car. "I'm sorry. We should have called you. And I'll explain everything. But first, let's get Katie inside. She needs her rest."

"I'll help." Will stepped forward.

Katie shook her head, frowning at him.

"No, I've got it," Frankie said, a harsh tone coming through with her words.

Frankie brushed past him, reaching to help Katie. He stepped back, giving them all space, then watched as the three of them slipped into the girls' cottage. He stood there beside the car, all alone. Excluded.

And why was Katie so mad at him, much less Frankie? What had changed?

He closed his eyes for a moment and suddenly felt very old. Defeated. Tired. It had been a long, stressful day, and it just kept spiraling downward.

CHAPTER 23

F rankie slept on the couch in the girls' cottage under the guise of not wanting to leave Katie's side no matter how much her daughter protested she was fine. But Katie did send her a sympathetic look when they made up the couch. Katie knew why she was staying here. There was no way she could go over and stay in the cottage with Will. By some kind of silent agreement, they'd decided not to tell Stacey about Will's cheating. Time enough to explain all that to her later.

She slipped out early the next morning after peeking in on Katie, who looked to be resting comfortably. She walked down to the water and kicked off her shoes, wading in the shallow rivulets of water from the ebbing tide. She bent over and picked up a shell that caught her eye, then noticed a large chip in it. Not as perfect as she'd thought. Nothing was as she thought it was these days. She tossed the shell back into the sea. "Fly free, little one."

If only she could fly free. Away from all her troubles. Away from reality. So much had changed in twenty-four hours. The excitement she'd felt after talking to Rose yesterday. The hope that maybe, just maybe, she and Will could find a way to make things work.

And then her fated trip into town. But maybe the universe was trying to protect her. Show her what kind of man Will was now. It was hard to deny it after seeing him with that woman. He'd been so happy, so delighted.

Fine, he could have his new woman.

"There you are." Rose came walking up to her. "I heard about Katie's accident. Is she okay?"

"She says she is. She actually looks fine. Ate a good meal last night. Just bruised a bit. Thank goodness for whoever invented airbags. I was just so terrified when I heard the news. Longest drive of my life heading to the hospital and not knowing what I'd find."

"I'm sure it was. I was just going to sit for a bit. Watch the rest of the sunrise. Want to join me?"

"Yes, that sounds nice." Suddenly, the idea of actually doing her morning walk seemed like it would take way too much energy. Everything seemed like too much energy. She wanted to crawl into bed, pull the covers over her head, and sleep for weeks.

They went to the ridge on the beach and settled on the sand.

"You okay? I guess yesterday really took it out of you." Rose looked at her closely.

"You have no idea. There was the accident... but then... Something else."

"You talked to Will?" Rose's raised her eyebrows.

"Not exactly. Not at all, actually. I went into town to find him." An annoying tear escaped, and she swiped at it. She'd thought she'd cried out all the tears she had yesterday. But this traitor escaped. "And when I found him, he was with another woman."

"What?"

"I saw him. Hugging her. Holding her hand. But the worst part was the look on his face. It was so obvious that he was so happy. I haven't seen him like that with me for years. He doesn't look at me that way."

Rose's forehead creased in a frown. "Are you sure? Here in Moonbeam?"

"I saw it. It's impossible to deny. Maybe he asked her to come here so he could see her? I don't know. I just know what I saw. And it was a man thrilled to see a woman."

"I'm so sorry. I was so sure you two would work things out. I just had a feeling."

"Looks like your feeling was wrong this time. I drove home yesterday after I saw him. Katie came to find me. And I told her what had happened, what I saw. Maybe I shouldn't have, but she would've found out soon enough. I shouldn't have let her leave, though. It's all my fault."

"Accidents happen. There's no way you could have known it would happen."

"But she came to find me to see why I left. If I just would have stayed here at the cottages instead of running off. I'm always running away when things get tough. Or if I had let her stay home with me when she got there. Then the accident wouldn't have happened."

"What are you going to do now?"

She trailed her fingers in the sand until she realized she was writing Will's name. She slashed her hand across the sand, erasing it, and turned to Rose. "I don't know. When I got home yesterday, I boxed up all his things. They're in the garage."

"What about the party?"

She sagged back, leaning on her arms. "The party. I'd forgotten all about it with all the chaos of yesterday. We'll have to contact everyone and cancel it. Not exactly how I wanted everyone to find out that we're splitting up."

"You don't have to give them that for the reason. You can just say you aren't feeling well."

"And that is sure the truth. I'm not. I'm mad. Sad. Furious. Worried about Katie. Unsure of the future."

"I'm sorry. I'm sure this is a very hard time for you." Rose's eyes shone with concern and sympathy.

"It all feels so impossible to get through. To get to the other side where I'll have some kind of life."

"Sometimes we just have to take what life sends us, even when we're not ready for it. And find our way to our new life."

"Oh, Rose. I'm sorry. I know you had to adjust to life without Emmett. That must have been so hard for you."

"It was hard, but I eventually made it through to the life I have now. You'll make it through all this, too."

"I know you're right. I just... I just don't know how I'm going to figure it all out. Like yesterday, I was wondering if I should sell our house. I don't need a big old house like that for just me. But there are so many memories there."

"You don't have to make that decision right now."

"No, I guess I don't. I actually don't feel like I'm thinking clearly enough right now to make *any* decisions."

Rose reached over and touched her hand. The hand that was still trying to obliterate the name she'd written in the sand. "Take your time. And take care of yourself while you're going through this. You're used to taking care of everyone else. You need to put yourself on the take-care-of list."

She squeezed Rose's hand. "I don't know how I would have made it through this week without you. I'm so glad we met. You've been a good listener and you've given me a lot of good advice."

"I'm glad I was here for you and could help in whatever little way I could."

Frankie pushed off the sand. "I think I should head up. Check in on Katie."

"Okay. But remember what I said. Take care of yourself, too."

Rose watched as Frankie headed up toward the cottages. What a rough time Frankie was having, but thank goodness her daughter would be okay. But to find out your husband was cheating on you by actually seeing him? And why would Will have invited his new woman to Moonbeam? Or had he just met her here and fallen for her? That part didn't really make sense. Maybe there was more to the story.

But Frankie was insistent about what she'd seen. The hugs, the handholding, the look on Will's face. It was a sad thing when a marriage fell apart. Sad for everyone. The couple, the kids. Even though their girls were grown, it would still rock their life. Her heart squeezed in sympathy for all of them and the road they had ahead.

She looked out over the water and saw a lone blue heron flying past, dotted against the pink clouds in the distance. She really should make her way back home one of these days. She couldn't really stay here forever, even though Violet said she wasn't taking any reservations for Rose's cottage until Rose was good and ready to move out. She just wasn't exactly sure when she would be ready to go back home.

Rose understood what Frankie meant about wondering if she should sell her house. Because she'd felt the same way since Emmett died. She certainly didn't need the big old house they'd lived in together. And he'd done so much to keep it up and looking nice. He was a born fixer. Could fix anything. She'd have to hire help to do the many things he had done for her. Loneliness clung to every corner of the house. She saw Emmett in the couch where he sat to read the evening paper. At the kitchen table. In the garage where he loved to putter as he fixed things. He was everywhere. Which was nice that she could feel him there, but also overwhelming and sad. She couldn't quite face going back home to that crushing loneliness.

But yet, the house also held wonderful memories. So many memories. How could she walk away from all of that? Leave the place she'd lived with Emmett for all those years?

She should take her own advice that she'd given Frankie. The decision didn't need to be made right now. She had time to figure it all out.

CHAPTER 24

Frankie walked up to the cottages and peeked in on Katie, who was still sound asleep. Katie rarely slept this late, but rest was good for her. And of course, Stacey was still sleeping, too. She'd never been an early riser.

Not wanting to wake the girls by putting on the coffee, she decided to head to the office and see if Violet had some made. She was sure she'd seen a pot on the counter the day they checked in.

She slipped out of the cottage and crossed the courtyard, heading to the office with high hopes for the coveted cup of coffee. She stopped abruptly when she saw Will standing at the edge of the parking area, talking to someone. As he stepped to one side, she gasped. It was that same woman. The petite blonde from town.

What was she doing here? She had some nerve to actually come to where they were staying. Had Will lost his mind? What was he doing slipping out to meet his new woman right here? What if the girls saw him? Wasn't their family in a big enough mess without this?

Before she had time to think, she sped across the distance, anger gathering inside her, and came up short right beside the couple.

"What are doing? Are you crazy?" She seriously wanted to reach out and punch him. Wipe that friendly, smiling look off his face as he talked to the woman. A look full of appreciation. She knew that look, though she hadn't seen it directed at her for years.

"Frankie?" His forehead crinkled.

"Really? It was bad enough you had her here to town on our family vacation. But you actually had her meet you at the cottages where we're staying? I don't even know you anymore."

Confusion covered his face. Not the look she was expecting. She at least deserved to see a look of guilt. Of shame.

"What are you talking about?" He glanced at the woman. "Oh, I'm sorry. Daisy, this is Frankie. Frankie, Daisy."

"You are actually going to stand there and introduce us?"

"I… um… yes?"

She turned to the woman. "And Daisy? You can have him. Good luck with that."

She spun on her heels and fled, forgetting all about the needed cup of coffee and taking care of Katie. She had to get away. All resolve to quit running away from conflict, from the hard stuff, was lost on her now. She fled back to the beach.

Will watched as Frankie sped away, then turned to Daisy. "I'm sorry. I don't know what that was about."

"She's probably just upset about your daughter's accident." She turned and reached into the open window of her car. "When I heard Katie had been in an accident, I thought maybe these would cheer her up." She pulled out a bouquet of brightly colored flowers.

"That was so nice of you." He reached for

the flowers, taking one glance over his shoulder just in time to see Frankie disappear on the beach.

"I always think flowers fix everything."

He wished it were that easy. That the lilacs he got for Frankie would fix everything. But he wasn't certain anything could fix them now. And what was up with Frankie's peculiar behavior? She was usually so nice and friendly with people she met. This had just been... strange.

"I'll make sure Katie gets them when she wakes up."

"Thank you. And if I can do anything to help, let me know."

"Thanks, Daisy. You've really been a great help this week." Not that he knew if Frankie would even accept the lilacs from him tomorrow on their anniversary.

Their anniversary. Wasn't that a joke? Had anyone called the people to cancel? Katie was usually the person to handle all the details. He should go and find her and see what he could do to help. Even if it meant calling all their friends to cancel the party and telling them why. Because he and Frankie were separating. He hadn't even moved out yet and was already feeling like everything was hopeless.

Daisy got in her car and pulled away, and he slowly made his way back to the cottages. Katie was sitting outside on her porch as he walked up. He climbed the steps and handed her the flowers. "From Daisy."

She reached for them. "That was sweet of her."

"She heard about the accident and thought they would cheer you up."

"I'm not sure anything will cheer me up."

He leaned against the railing across from her. "Katie, what's wrong? You're acting all mad at me. Did I do something?"

She shot him an angry glance. "You did. You hurt Mom."

"I know we're having trouble. It's nothing I did deliberately. And I've tried to change."

She laughed a shallow laugh. "Change. That's one thing to call it."

"Why are you mad at me? And what did your mother say when you went to see her yesterday? Why did she leave?"

"She said that if you thought about it, you'd figure it out."

"Come on, Katydid. Don't play games. Not now. No riddles. Just tell me what's wrong."

"Mom found out that you're..." Her eyes blazed. "That you're cheating on her. How could you, Dad?"

"I'm not cheating on your mother." Confusion crashed down on him, which seemed his normal way of feeling these days.

"There's no use denying it. She saw you. In town. Yesterday morning. With another woman. You hugged her and held her hand, and Mom said you looked absolutely thrilled to see this woman. Very excited and happy."

He frowned. "I didn't meet another woman in town." He thought back over his day yesterday. He hadn't seen anyone but... Daisy. No, had Frankie thought there was something between him and Daisy? If so, that would explain how mad she'd been just a moment ago when he was talking to Daisy. The strange way she'd acted.

"And your timing was terrible, Dad. Picked a lousy time to cheat on Mom. She said yesterday she was looking for you to try and talk to you. That she was even planning on asking you not to move out."

He stared at Katie. "Frankie was going to ask me to stay?"

"I don't know everything she was thinking, but I do know she's beyond furious with you now."

He could only imagine Frankie's thoughts if she believed he was seeing someone else. *Daisy.*

"I've got to go find Frankie. I'll explain everything later, Katydid. But your mother is wrong. I didn't cheat on her. But I have to go find her. Right away. And straighten all this out. No wonder she was so mad at me. But I didn't cheat. I never would."

She looked at him doubtfully.

"Really, it's not what it seems. But I have to find Frankie and explain." He rushed down the steps and headed in the direction he'd seen her disappear.

Now, if only Frankie would actually listen to him.

How could she have thought he was cheating on her? After all this time? Didn't she know him better than that? But if she truly believed it, he was heading to face one truly ticked-off woman. Frankie wouldn't even want to hear him out. But she was going to have to. He had to straighten this all out.

And had she really been ready to ask him to stay? After all this time of demanding that he moved out? A tiny grain of hope grew inside him.

But first, he had to face her.

CHAPTER 25

Will rushed toward the beach, then paused and looked in each direction. Then he saw her. Sitting on the beach with Rose. He raced up to them, and Frankie looked up at him with reddened, swollen eyes, her face covered in tears.

"Go away, Will. I don't want to see you."

He dropped to his knees beside her. "Please, Frankie. You have to listen to me. I didn't cheat on you. I never would."

Rose looked over at him for a moment as if reading his expression, then nodded slightly as she got up from the sand. "I'll just leave you two to talk a bit."

"No… Rose." Frankie reached out and took the woman's hand.

"Frankie, I think it's time you two had a nice long talk. Listen to what he has to say. And… don't run away from your problems."

Frankie watched Rose walk away before turning back to him. "I have nothing to say to you. Please leave."

"I'm not going. Not until you listen to me."

She turned and stared out at the water as if ignoring him, but not before he saw the anger boiling in her eyes.

Oh, his Frankie was mad. Very mad.

"Frankie, listen to me."

She didn't bother to look at him. "I asked you to leave. I don't want to talk."

"We need to talk. What's this nonsense about me cheating on you? Don't you know me well enough to know I'd never do that?"

"I thought I knew you. Well, I used to know you. But now? No… I don't know you at all."

"Sure you do. You know I'm the man who loves you more than anyone else in the world. The man who would never cheat on you. Frankie, what you saw was me talking to Daisy. She owns the flower shop in town, Beach

Blooms. She found… something for me. Something I wanted for our anniversary."

Frankie turned to him, tilted her head to the side, and frowned.

"She found… lilacs."

"Lilacs?" Her eyes widened as a stunned expression settled on her face.

"Yes, I wanted to give you lilacs for our anniversary. I know you love them."

"But you hugged her. You held her hand."

"I did hug her in my excitement. And I guess I did reach out and shake her hand to thank her. But that's all it was. I swear."

"That's all it was? You were trying to surprise me with lilacs?" Her voice was so soft he could barely hear it.

"Yes. But I guess they won't be much of a surprise now."

He took her hand in his. She stared down at their hands but didn't pull away. "I guess… I guess I just jumped to the wrong conclusion. You just looked so happy."

"I *was* happy. Happy to be able to surprise *you* with lilacs. Hoping you would enjoy them. That they'd make you happy."

"That was… a nice thing to do." A fresh

tear rolled down her cheek. "You weren't seeing her? You haven't moved on to someone else?"

He reached over and brushed away the tear with his thumb. "I can never move on from you, Frankie. You're a part of me. And Katie said you were coming to find me yesterday. To ask me to stay."

"I... I was. And I know I've been asking you to move out. It's just that I'm scared..."

"What are you scared of? Not of me?" His heart lurched just thinking of Frankie being afraid of him.

"I'm scared if I let down my guard, and we try again, that I'll just be hurt again. I don't think my heart can take that."

"I'm not going to hurt you. I swear we'll work all this out. I promise."

"I've just felt so invisible the last few years. You hurry in from work and off to your den to work again. We don't talk. We've drifted so far apart. And I think I've just wrapped up my heart so it wouldn't hurt so much. I'm not sure I'll be able to let all that go."

He brushed back a lock of her hair, his fingers trailing across her cheek. How he'd missed that. Touching her. "Frankie, I'm so sorry. I know I didn't put much effort into us. I took us for granted. Took you for granted. And that's not right. I don't blame you for pulling away and asking me to leave. But, please, let me stay. Let's talk and work things out. Just tell me what needs to change."

Frankie stared at Will, at the earnest look on his face. Now was the time to tell him everything. Tell him how she felt. She swallowed and took a deep breath. "Like I said, I feel invisible. I know I'm gray and pudgy and not in good shape. You don't look at me like you used to. I can't remember the last time you kissed me."

"Oh, Frankie. I'm so sorry. I shouldn't have let it get this far. To fall into a pattern of complacency. That was wrong. I should have told you that I love you. I do, you know. I think you're still so attractive. So sexy. Yes, we might be older now, but I think age looks good on you."

A small laugh escaped her. "Now I think you're sweet-talking me."

"And would that be wrong? I want to sweet-talk you. I want to tell you how much you mean to me. How much I love you. How very sorry I am."

The honesty in his eyes said it all. A bit of hope began to grow. She touched his face, and his eyes glistened. "And I'm sorry, too. I should have tried harder to talk to you. I know when we tried talking before I got angry and walked away. I shouldn't have."

"We're talking now."

She swallowed again and continued. "I felt… unattractive, but that's not all. It was like my whole life up until a few years ago was about you and the girls. What you all needed. And then you all deserted me and there was just… nothing left."

"Ah, Frankie, I'm sorry you felt that way. You were amazing raising the girls, and you've always been there for me. I guess we all just took that for granted."

"You know how I'd take those part-time jobs when the girls were younger, but then something always came up to conflict with the job. And I'd just leave the job so I could be there for the girls and you."

He frowned. "You did do that. Quite a few

times. I shouldn't have let that happen. We should have figured out a different way to make it work out."

"And now I think… well, I want to find something to do that fulfills me. Not some part-time receptionist or a checkout person. Oh, and I'll never go back to bookkeeping. Hated that job. But I did put a call into my friend, Mary. She's running the children's foundation now. Maybe I could work there. Or even volunteer."

"I swear I'll adapt my schedule around yours if you want to go back to work. You've supported me for enough years." He squeezed her hand. "And about the moving out? Can I stay?"

Her pulse quickened as she stared into his eyes and slowly nodded. "Yes, you can stay. I think you should."

"Perfect." His face broke into a boyish, silly grin, then grew serious. "And if you want me to still stay in the guest room for a bit, that's fine. We'll take everything slowly. At whatever speed you want."

She looked away, heat crossing her cheeks. "Ah… about that. Your stuff is all in the garage. I kind of boxed it all up."

He threw back his head and laughed. "I don't care about that. I don't. I just want…" He paused and took both her hands in his. "I just want a chance to prove to you that things will be different. To give us a chance."

"I'd like that, too."

"And… you know how you said you couldn't remember the last time I kissed you?"

She nodded as her pulse raced.

"I think we should fix that." He leaned in closer and reached up to cup her face. He kissed her tenderly and wrapped his other arm around her, pulling her close.

Her heart pounded as his lips met hers. So wanted. So familiar, like a long-forgotten memory suddenly springing into her consciousness.

When he finally pulled away, she swore she saw tears glistening in his eyes. "That was just the first of many, Frankie. Many, many."

"Then I think you should try it again, so I believe you."

He threw back his head and laughed, then jumped to his feet and reached down to pull her up with him. He scooped her up to twirl her around and around, just like he used to when they were so much younger. Then he set her down and kissed her again. And once more for good measure.

She finally pulled away. "You know what we have to do?"

"Besides, move all my stuff back in?" He winked at her.

"Besides that. We need to talk to the girls and make sure they don't cancel our anniversary party."

"Absolutely. Good plan. I can't wait to celebrate forty years with you. And I plan on many more years to come." He nodded. "But one thing. You never answered me about whether you want me to move my things back into the guest room... or into our room."

Her heart crackled in her chest, and she wanted to do the safe thing. Have him move back to the guest room. Take things slow. Protect herself in case things didn't work out. And yet... "Ah, I guess you should move back into our room."

He reached out and took her hand, pulling her close. "I swear I won't let you get hurt again, Frankie. Won't ever take you for granted. You'll see." He pulled her into his arms and held her against him. "I've missed you." He kissed the top of her head while his strong arms encircled her.

"I've missed you, too." She leaned her cheek against his chest, feeling his heartbeat. There was nowhere else she'd rather be than right here in his arms.

CHAPTER 26

Katie went inside the cottage and found Stacey sitting at the table, sipping coffee. Her sister looked up and glared at her. "So are any of you going to tell me what's going on?"

She sighed as she went over and poured herself a cup of coffee, then sat across from her sister. It was time Stacey heard the truth. Hopefully, she wouldn't find a way to make this all about her. "So, Mom saw Dad with another woman."

"No way." Stacey's eyes widened.

"Yes, here in town. But then when I confronted Dad, he swore he didn't cheat on Mom. That he never would."

"Isn't that what men always say when they get caught?"

She knew Stacey was talking from experience from her brief marriage, but still, her father had looked so sincere when he said he hadn't cheated on their mom.

"Anyway, Dad went to go find Mom and talk to her."

"Good luck with that. You said she was polishing all the silver. She only does that when she's furious." Stacey got up and poured another cup of coffee, then returned. "So that's why Mom left?"

"It was. She couldn't bear to be around Dad after seeing him."

"Do you think she'll believe him? That nothing is going on?"

"I'm not sure."

"Do *you* believe him?"

She let out another long sigh. "I'm not sure. I want to believe him, but Mom did see him."

"This is really messed up." Stacey scowled. "I just want everything to go back the way it was. This is horrible."

"It is. And now we have to call everyone we

invited to the party and tell them it's canceled. Figure out an excuse to give them."

Stacey looked at her for a moment, then shook her head. "You should do that. You're better at that kind of stuff than I am. You'll find the right words."

"You can't make me do all the calls." She swallowed back her anger. "You have to help. I *need* your help."

"I've got an appointment in an hour to get my nails done." Stacey stood, then went over to put her cup in the sink. "Anyway, you'll figure out a way to smooth it over with everyone." She headed down the hall.

She shouldn't be surprised at Stacey's refusal to help. It was par for the course. Just the way she was. But still, it disappointed her that when she'd actually said the words that she needed Stacey's help, her sister refused.

She retrieved her laptop, then sat back down, opening the computer to find the note with the list of invitees.

Perfect. Just perfect. She had addresses for all of them, but not all the phone numbers. She'd need to get those from Mom's phone.

She reached for her phone to call her mom when a text came in from her mother.

Don't cancel the party. We'll explain later.

And she wasn't sure if that was good news or bad news. Had Mom forgiven Dad? Or had he really convinced her that he wasn't cheating? But Mom had seen him. Was there really a good explanation for what she saw?

Well, the good news was she didn't have a day of making phone calls.

"Stacey, the party's back on," she called out.

Stacey walked back into the front room. "It is?"

"Yep. Don't know what happened, but Mom just texted."

"Looks like we won't have to make all those calls, then."

We weren't going to make them…

Melody looked up to see Ethan heading toward her in the cafe.

"Hey, you." His face broke into a wide smile.

"Hi, Ethan. A little late for breakfast, aren't you?"

"Yeah, I grabbed toast at home. I had errands to run in town."

She didn't want to admit she'd been disappointed when he hadn't come in this morning. But that was silly. She'd just seen him last night when he came by the cafe to walk her home after the restaurant closed.

"So I ran into the Jenkins twins today." Ethan shook his head. "Evidently, the whole town knows we went out on a date."

"They were here at the cafe yesterday, too. Asking a lot of questions."

"They asked me how the date went," he said with a trace of amusement.

"And what did you say?"

"I said it was the best date ever." He winked. "Then they asked me how I felt about you."

"They did? What did you say to that?" Her pulse quickened as she waited for his answer.

He reached out and took her hand. "I said you were very special to me."

Her pulse skittered through her veins. "I'm special to you?"

"Mel, I've cared about you for a long time. I was just waiting for it to be the right time for you. I know you've had a rough time with losing John. I don't want to replace him. I just want to be a part of your life." He paused, searching her face. "And… I'd like to be more than friends. Still friends, but more."

"I do want to go out with you again. I look forward to our picnic. But… but I can't make you any promises. I'm just not sure how all this is going to work out."

He dipped his chin, nodding slightly. "That's okay. You can take all the time in the world to figure things out. I'm just glad you agreed to go out with me. And go out with me again on Sunday. We can take it slow."

"Yes, that's good."

"I'd do anything for you, Mel. Anything." With one last long look, he turned and headed out of the cafe.

She stood there for a moment, conflicted. She wanted to ask him to stay and have some coffee, sit with her. Yet, she'd told him she wanted to take things slowly.

She walked back into the kitchen and Evelyn looked up. "Hey, you okay?"

"I don't know."

Evelyn walked over, looking concerned. "What's wrong?"

"Ethan just said he's cared about me for a long time. And he told the Jenkins twins that I'm special to him."

Evelyn laughed. "Well, then the whole town will know. Might as well plaster the news on a billboard."

She sank onto a stool by the counter. "And you know what the funny thing is?"

"No, what?"

"I think I don't care if the whole town knows."

Evelyn grinned, shook her head, and went back over to where a pie crust lay spread out on the counter. "Well, if Jackie and Jillian know, then everyone will."

"And he said we could take it as slow as I need things."

"That's good."

"Is it?" She cocked her head. Did she want things to go slowly? Or did she want... did she want him to kiss her?

Evelyn laughed. "Good thing you have another date with him, so you can sort this all out."

"Right, a good thing." She couldn't wait for her date on Sunday. She had all these mixed feelings, but the only way to sort them out was to spend time with Ethan. She jumped up, shoving her jumbled thoughts far away. Evelyn was right. She'd sort it out tomorrow. "Here, let me help you. I'll peel the apples."

CHAPTER 27

F rankie couldn't have asked for a more perfect night. Their pre-anniversary night. They had dinner at The Cabot Hotel, where she'd originally thought they were having their anniversary dinner. That was before she found out about the not-so-surprise party the girls planned.

Will explained everything to the girls about Daisy and the lilacs. And she tried to tamp down her guilt for ever thinking he would cheat on her. He held her hand under the table, and they all laughed and talked and had the best family dinner ever. This was a night she thought they'd never have again. A family night where they all could just relax and enjoy themselves. Where there was no tension crackling between her and Will.

When they returned to Blue Heron Cottages, they all headed across the courtyard. The stars twinkled above and Will held her hand as they slowly walked across the grass. Contentment wrapped around her like a favorite quilt.

Katie glanced over at them. "Ah… Stacey and I are going to call it a night. We've got a few things to do to get ready for tomorrow."

"We do?" Stacey asked.

"Yes, we do," Katie said firmly as she took her sister's arm and dragged her toward their cottage, whispering something in her ear.

Stacey looked back at them and grinned. "Yes, we have stuff to do. Lots of stuff." The girls disappeared inside.

Will held her hand as they climbed the stairs to their cottage. "It was a good night, wasn't it?" he asked as he opened the door.

"It was a wonderful night."

Will closed the door behind them. "Want a nightcap? Some wine?"

"No, I think I'm fine."

He stood there in the warm glow of the lamplight and looked at her. Really looked at her. Like he hadn't in a very long time. Like he was drinking in every detail. A warmth and happiness swept through her. He was looking at her just like he used to so very long ago.

"Ah… Frankie." He took three quick steps until he was right in front of her. "You're so beautiful. I've missed you so much."

She touched his face, trailing her finger along the stubbly growth of his evening whiskers. He'd always had a heavy beard and often shaved again in the evening if they were going out.

"Sorry, should have shaved," he said as if reading her thoughts. Reading her thought just like he used to.

"No, that's okay." She ran her fingers across his other cheek, and he captured her hand in his, kissing it lightly. A thrill ran through her, stirring feelings she'd hidden for so long. Ignored for so long. Wished for…

"I can't get enough of you. Talking to you. Seeing you. Holding you. I've missed you so much. It's like a chunk of me was missing." His eyes blazed with a smoky longing. The same look she was certain her face held.

"In that case…" And she was willing to risk this because she'd missed him so much. Missed the old Will. The Will who seemed to be standing before her right now. "In that case… maybe we should… you know…" She looked down the hallway toward the bedroom where she was staying, then looked at him, feeling the blush creep across her face.

His eyes widened, and he grinned. "Well, Francine Winters. You frisky woman. Were you getting ready to ask me… to bed?"

"If you want to…" Her heart pounded as she stared into his eyes. The eyes smoldering with desire. Desire for *her*.

"I want nothing more." He swept her up in his arms and carried her down the hallway, then set her gently down on the bed.

She reached up and tugged on his shoulders, pulling him down closer.

And just like that, her world started to fall back into place and the tiny glow of hope expanded into a flame of certainty.

She and Will would figure things out. They would make their way back to each other.

Because there was no one in the whole world she'd rather spend her days with. And her nights.

He kissed her gently and reached over and turned out the light.

CHAPTER 28

Frankie was late taking her walk the next morning because she couldn't pull herself away from Will. From his kisses. His strong arms. From the hope that things were all going to work out. Yes, they still had a lot to sort out, but she had every belief that they would. That things would change. Maybe even be better than before. The two of them could do this together.

They sat together, sipping coffee, until she finally set her cup on the table. "I want to go find Rose. Let her know... let her know that things worked out."

Will leaned over and kissed her. "Hurry back. I'll miss you."

She laughed as she walked out the door and headed to the beach. When she saw Rose, she waved and raced over. Rose grinned as Frankie dropped down beside her.

"Well, that's a different woman than the one I talked to yesterday."

She laughed. "It is. I am. You were right. I needed to talk to Will. Tell him how I felt. And I was wrong… He wasn't having an affair. He was just talking to the florist, who found lilacs for me. He was excited she'd found them. Lilacs are my favorite flower."

"Daisy? He was talking to Daisy?" Rose's lips slipped into a grin. "And did you tell him how you've been feeling?"

"I did. And admitted part of this is my fault. I should have talked to him long ago. Not just gotten mad and walked away every time, trying to protect myself. I should have talked to him and explained exactly how his actions made me feel. How lonely I was."

"I'm glad you two seem to have worked things out. Or at least you're starting to work things out."

"We are. And there's something I wanted to ask you."

"Ask away."

"Would you come to our anniversary party tonight? I feel like you're part of the reason we're actually having it."

"I'd love to."

"Perfect." She jumped up. "I've lots to do today, but I wanted to make sure I saw you and invited you. I'll see you tonight."

"I'll see you tonight."

She turned and headed back to the cottage. She missed Will and laughed at herself. She felt like a teenager with a crush who couldn't get enough of her boyfriend.

When she got back to the cottage, there was no sign of Will, but she heard the water running. He must be taking a shower. A mischievous grin crept across her face. Hm… maybe she needed a shower too… And she headed to the bathroom to surprise him.

Katie and Stacey stood in the courtyard, setting up for the party. At least she was setting up for the party. Stacey was mostly just kind of standing around. Stacey set up a chair, and Katie went over and moved it.

She couldn't miss the sigh that escaped Stacey.

"What?" She turned to her sister. "You've hardly helped with a thing." Katie snatched the chair Stacey was unfolding and set it with the chair she'd just moved. A nice little seating area with six chairs. Perfect. Couldn't Stacey see that putting the chairs in a line didn't make it easy for people to have conversations?

"Of course not. You don't really let people help you. You like to make the decisions and do things your way. It's always been like that. You don't listen to me. You still treat me like I'm your little kid sister and have no right to my own opinion on things. A right to do things my way." Stacey's eyes flashed with annoyance.

She stopped unfolding the chair and stared at her sister. "No, I don't."

"Yes, you do." Stacey eyed her. "You don't accept we're different. That I do things differently than you. But that doesn't mean I'm doing things wrong. Living my life wrong. You're always so judgmental."

"No, I'm not." She set the chair down. Was

she, though? She did like things to be done a certain way, and she did judge Stacey for the way she lived her life. Certainly not how she'd live her life.

"And I'm tired of it. Trying to always be who you want me to be. And if I do help... you just redo whatever I did." Stacey eyed the chairs.

"That's not true."

"It is. I'll just let you finish this because anything I do will be wrong. Just like yesterday when you wanted help making all those calls. But... I wouldn't have said things the way you wanted me to. I know I wouldn't. And you'd get aggravated at me like you always do." Stacey whirled away and headed toward the cottage.

The truth to Stacey's words surged through her, filling her with remorse. She jogged over to catch up with her and grabbed her sister's arm. "No, don't go. I'm sorry."

Stacey turned to look at her. "Sorry about what?"

"About... everything. Maybe you do have a point. I do like things done my way and maybe I am a bit judgmental."

"A bit?" Stacey cocked her head.

"Well, okay. A lot. And I'm sorry. You have every right to live your life just like you want to."

"Just like you have every right to live your life so straight-laced and organized that you're never spontaneous."

"I am too spontaneous."

"Name the last time you did something that wasn't all planned out."

"Well... I..." Then she grinned at her sister. "I didn't plan to be in an accident."

Stacey rolled her eyes, then a sly smile crept across her lips. "So, you're okay if *I* put the flowers out that Daisy brought over?"

"What?" She hesitated a moment, thinking of her carefully laid out plan of where to put each bouquet, but recovered. "Sure, of course. Put them anywhere you want."

"And you won't move them?"

"Of course not. I'll go work on setting up the table for the food."

They walked back over and Stacey started placing the flowers around. Not where she would have placed them, but they looked good enough. Though that big arrangement should really be on the main table...

Stacey's laugh rang across the distance. "This is killing you, isn't it?"

"No, not at all." And with that, she was determined to not move the flowers even an inch. Even if they all were in the wrong places.

"Come on, Katie. Let's go get dressed. You can angst over which dress you're going to wear."

"I'm not going to angst…" Though, she knew she would because she still wasn't sure which dress was more appropriate.

"I'll pick for you," Stacey said as they entered the cottage.

"Well…" She took a deep breath. "Okay."

Stacey laughed. "Nah, you go ahead and angst. I expect nothing less from you on the *big* decision like which dress to wear."

"No, you pick. I'm sure that will be fine. Perfect even."

Stacey disappeared and came out with a dress with tiny navy pinstripes and a round neckline. "This one… but not with the navy shoes you brought." She whipped her hands from behind her back. "With these red flats."

"But I bought the navy shoes specifically to go with the dress."

Stacey eyed her. "And?"

"And the red flats will be perfect." She took the outfit from Stacey and headed back to her room.

"You'll look fabulous," Stacey called out as she disappeared into her own room.

CHAPTER 29

"You ready for this?" Will stood in the front room of their cottage looking devilishly handsome in his crisp gray slacks and button-down shirt with tiny gray pinstripes.

She put on her earrings and looked in the mirror. "I think so."

He walked up behind her and kissed her neck. "Have I told you how beautiful you look lately?"

He had. Yesterday. And last night. And even this morning in the shower. She couldn't help but bask in his compliments, enjoying his attention.

She kissed him lightly on the lips. "Let's go have this party."

Will held her hand through all of the anniversary party. Welcoming their friends. Listening to toasts and stories their friends told about knowing them. Strands of small white lights crisscrossed the area, illuminating the courtyard as the sky broke into a brilliant display of oranges and purples, a magical sunset.

Her friend Mary came up to her. "Oh, Francine, I got your email. It was perfect timing. We just lost our event coordinator, and you used to do such a great job with our events. If that's something you might be interested in, let's talk when you get back home."

"I'd love that."

"Great, call me next week. And happy anniversary you two lovebirds."

Lovebirds. Who would have thought at the start of this vacation that she'd ever consider herself a lovebird with Will, yet she did.

Will squeezed her hand. "And I promise I'll work my schedule around yours if you take this job. No more changing everything for me. It's time that Frankie got her chance to shine."

Rose walked up to them. "Don't you two

look like the perfect couple? And Frankie, you look lovely."

"Thank you, Rose." She took Rose's hand. "I owe so much to you."

"Ah, you did all this on your own. Found your way back to each other." Rose turned to Will. "And I hope you two can remember how special you are to each other. Appreciate what you have."

"Oh, I'll never forget it." Will wrapped his arm around her shoulders and her heart swelled with love.

"That's good. You should never take a love like yours for granted." Rose smiled, then disappeared into the crowd of their friends.

Will kissed her. "I've got to do something." He stepped away and moved up near the front of the courtyard. "Excuse me." His voice rose over the talk of the crowd.

The noise died down.

"I'd like to make a toast to my beautiful wife. We've had forty good years. Wonderful daughters who have brought us so much joy." He held out his hand to her, and she walked up and took it, a bottomless peace and happiness surging through her. "I can't imagine going through this life with anyone except my Francine. She makes every moment worth living, makes it special. And I plan on making sure she knows how much I love her and how special she is... every day for the rest of our lives."

She fought back the tears crowding her eyes.

He held up his glass. "To Frankie. The most wonderful woman in the world."

"To Frankie," the crowd said.

Katie walked up to them and raised her glass, then paused for a moment and motioned to Stacey. Stacey walked up beside her. "Go for it, Stacey. Make a toast for us."

Stacey looked surprised, then raised her glass. "To my parents, the irrepressible Mr. and Mrs. Winters. May they have many more years of wedded bliss."

"To Frankie and Will." Their friends raised their glasses again.

"You look beautiful." Will leaned close to her. "I've got a little present for you. Let's go over where it's not so crowded."

"More than my lilacs?" She looked over to where the lilacs sat in a vase on the table. "We weren't supposed to get presents, remember?"

She followed him over to the edge of the crowd.

"I know, but I wanted you to have this. It's not much, but…"

He handed her a small box he evidently wrapped himself, with crooked paper and a lopsided bow. And no one could have done a more perfect job as far as she was concerned. She unwrapped the box, opened it, and gasped. "Oh, Will. It's perfect. Just like the one you gave me all those years ago."

He grinned at her. "I hoped you would like it."

She slipped the bracelet of lilac beads onto her wrist. "It's lovely." She stood up on tiptoe to kiss him. "Thank you."

He leaned close to her. "I'm glad you like it. I can't imagine my life without you. I want so many more anniversaries together."

"I do, too."

"I promise I'll never let you feel unappreciated again. I can't imagine my life without you in it. You mean everything to me. And you are so beautiful tonight. So very beautiful."

And she glowed with his words. She reached

up and tugged him close for a kiss. "You mean everything to me, too. And I plan on toasting every anniversary with you right by my side."

She knew they still had things to work out. That they might have difficulties. But she truly believed they would work things out. Together.

"Hey, most of the crowd has left." He nudged her gently. "Do you think we could, you know… slip away to our cottage and… uh… have our own private little celebration?" He sent her an impish grin.

"Well, Mr. Winters, are you asking me to… bed?"

"That I am, woman. That I am."

He took her hand, and they went to say goodnight to the girls and headed back to their cottage. She was hopelessly in love with this man. She always would be.

"Me, too, Frankie. I'm hopelessly in love with you."

He'd read her mind with that connection they used to share and did again. And just like that, they were in sync once more.

I hope you enjoyed Frankie and Will's story. Next up is Daisy's story, Flower Shop on Magnolia. She starts to fall for Jack… then finds out there's no way that relationship will work.

Or will it?

Oh, and Melody and Ethan are *still* trying to figure things out! And we're still learning more about Rose…

As always, thanks for reading my stories. I truly appreciate all of my readers. Thank you.

ALSO BY KAY CORRELL

COMFORT CROSSING ~ THE SERIES

The Shop on Main - Book One

The Memory Box - Book Two

The Christmas Cottage - A Holiday Novella (Book 2.5)

The Letter - Book Three

The Christmas Scarf - A Holiday Novella (Book 3.5)

The Magnolia Cafe - Book Four

The Unexpected Wedding - Book Five

The Wedding in the Grove (crossover short story between series - Josephine and Paul from The Letter.)

LIGHTHOUSE POINT ~ THE SERIES

Wish Upon a Shell - Book One

Wedding on the Beach - Book Two

Love at the Lighthouse - Book Three

Cottage near the Point - Book Four

Return to the Island - Book Five

Bungalow by the Bay - Book Six

Christmas Comes to Lighthouse Point - Book Seven

CHARMING INN ~ Return to Lighthouse Point

One Simple Wish - Book One

Two of a Kind - Book Two

Three Little Things - Book Three

Four Short Weeks - Book Four

Five Years or So - Book Five

Six Hours Away - Book Six

Charming Christmas - Book Seven

SWEET RIVER ~ THE SERIES

A Dream to Believe in - Book One

A Memory to Cherish - Book Two

A Song to Remember - Book Three

A Time to Forgive - Book Four

A Summer of Secrets - Book Five

A Moment in the Moonlight - Book Six

MOONBEAM BAY ~ THE SERIES

The Parker Women - Book One

The Parker Cafe - Book Two

A Heather Parker Original - Book Three

The Parker Family Secret - Book Four

Grace Parker's Peach Pie - Book Five

The Perks of Being a Parker - Book Six

BLUE HERON COTTAGES ~ THE SERIES

Memories of the Beach - Book One

Walks along the Shore - Book Two

Bookshop near the Coast - Book Three

Restaurant on the Wharf - Book Four

Lilacs by the Sea - Book Five

Flower Shop on Magnolia - Book Six

Plus more to come!

WIND CHIME BEACH ~ A stand-alone novel

INDIGO BAY ~ Save by getting Kay's complete collection of stories previously published separately in the multi-author Indigo Bay series. The three stories are all interconnected.

Sweet Days by the Bay - the collection

ABOUT THE AUTHOR

Kay Correll is a USA Today bestselling author of sweet, heartwarming stories that are a cross between women's fiction and contemporary romance. She is known for her charming small towns, quirky townsfolk, and the enduring strong friendships between the women in her books.

Kay splits her time between the southwest coast of Florida and the Midwest of the U.S. and can often be found out and about with her camera, taking a myriad of photographs, often incorporating them into her book covers. When not lost in her writing or photography, she can be found spending time with her ever-supportive husband, knitting, or playing with her puppies - a cavalier who is too cute for his own good and a naughty but adorable Australian shepherd. Their five boys are all grown now and while she misses the rowdy boy-noise chaos, she is thoroughly enjoying her empty nest years.

Learn more about Kay and her books at kaycorrell.com

While you're there, sign up for her newsletter to hear about new releases, sales, and giveaways.

WHERE TO FIND ME:
kaycorrell.com
authorcontact@kaycorrell.com

Join my Facebook Reader Group. We have lots of fun and you'll hear about sales and new releases first!
www.facebook.com/groups/KayCorrell/

I love to hear from my readers. Feel free to contact me at authorcontact@kaycorrell.com

facebook.com/KayCorrellAuthor

instagram.com/kaycorrell

pinterest.com/kaycorrellauthor

amazon.com/author/kaycorrell

bookbub.com/authors/kay-correll